MW00775578

$L \frac{9}{20}$
lA

BREAKTHROUGH

What Reviewers Say About Kris Bryant's Work

Forget Me Not

"Told in the first person, from Grace's point of view, we are privy to Grace's inner musings and her vulnerabilities. ...Bryant crafts clever wording to infuse Grace with a sharp-witted personality, which clearly covers her insecurities. ...This story is filled with loving familial interactions, caring friends, romantic interludes and tantalizing sex scenes. The dialogue, both among the characters and within Grace's head, is refreshing, original, and sometimes comical. *Forget Me Not* is a fresh perspective on a romantic theme, and an entertaining read."—*Lambda Literary Review*

Shameless

"...She has a way of giving insight into the other main protagonist by using a few clever techniques and involving the secondary characters to add back-stories and extra pieces of important information. The pace of the book was excellent, it was never rushed but I was never bored or waiting for a chapter to finish... this epilogue made my heart swell to the point I almost lunged off the sofa to do a happy dance."—*Les Rêveur*

Whirlwind Romance

"Ms. Bryant's descriptions were written with such passion and colourful detail that you could feel the tension and the excitement along with the characters..."—*Inked Rainbow Reviews*

Taste

"[*Taste*] is an excellent traditional romance, well written, well conceived and well put together. Kris Bryant has given us a lovely warm-hearted story about two real human beings with whom we can genuinely engage. There is no melodrama, no overblown angst, just two women with an instant attraction who have to decide first, how to deal with it and second, how much it's worth."—*Lesbian Reading Room*

"*Taste* is a student/teacher romance set in a culinary school. If the premise makes you wonder whether this book will make you want to eat something tasty, the answer is: yes."—*The Lesbian Review*

Jolt

"[*Jolt*] is a magnificent love story. Two women hurt by their previous lovers and each in their own way trying to make sense out of life and times. When they meet at a gay and lesbian friendly summer camp, they both feel as if lightening has struck. This is so beautifully involving, I have already reread it twice. Amazing!" —*Rainbow Book Reviews*

Touch

"The sexual chemistry in this book is off the hook. Kris Bryant writes my favorite sex scenes in lesbian romantic fiction."—*Les Reveur*

Visit us at www.boldstrokesbooks.com

By the Author

Jolt

Whirlwind Romance

Just Say Yes: The Proposal

Taste

Forget Me Not

Touch

Breakthrough

Writing as Brit Ryder:

Shameless

BREAKTHROUGH

by
Kris Bryant

2018

BREAKTHROUGH
© 2018 By Kris Bryant. All Rights Reserved.

ISBN 13: 978-1-63555-179-2

This Trade Paperback Original Is Published By
Bold Strokes Books, Inc.
P.O. Box 249
Valley Falls, NY 12185

First Edition: May 2018

THIS IS A WORK OF FICTION. NAMES, CHARACTERS, PLACES, AND
INCIDENTS ARE THE PRODUCT OF THE AUTHOR'S IMAGINATION OR
ARE USED FICTITIOUSLY. ANY RESEMBLANCE TO ACTUAL PERSONS,
LIVING OR DEAD, BUSINESS ESTABLISHMENTS, EVENTS, OR LOCALES
IS ENTIRELY COINCIDENTAL.

THIS BOOK, OR PARTS THEREOF, MAY NOT BE REPRODUCED IN ANY
FORM WITHOUT PERMISSION.

Credits
Editor: Ashley Tillman
Production Design: Susan Ramundo
Cover Design By Sheri (graphicartist2020@hotmail.com)

Acknowledgments

I have a wonderful family of friends, other writers, and readers who constantly encourage me to tell my stories. A heartfelt thanks to Radclyffe and Bold Strokes Books for publishing my books. There is so much that goes on behind the scenes, so many women involved that without their hard work, these books wouldn't get into the hands of our readers.

How I am able to start a book and finish it is based solely on my friends pushing me (and looming deadlines). There are so many women to thank—KB Draper and Hot Stacy for being my cheerleaders and only a twenty-minute drive away when I need encouragement; Megan Ullrich and Maggie Cummings for boosting my ego and just being the coolest "they" in my life.

There are wonderful writers who inspire me to do my best—Friz, Carol, Fiona, Melissa, Georgia, Cindy, Heather, Dena, and hundreds more. We have proofers and readers who make our works successful. Thank you, Kathy, Sue, Nadine, Val, Karen, Kaz, Heather, Paula, and thousands of others who read our books, get the word out, and feel just as passionate about our stories as we do. Reviews are so important to our success. Thank you TLR, Tara, Sheena, Anna, April, Amy, Rachael, Lambda Literary, and the publications who push our names and reviews. Lesfic is a very important part of the literary world, and it's growing bigger every day with every book that is written, published, and recommended. Thank you.

I owe so much to my editor, Ashley, for pointing out mistakes I never see, and for polishing my stories to a nice shine. She makes me cooler than I really am.

I am fortunate to have my dreams come true.

Dedication

To Deb

Alaska was one of the best trips of my life! Thank you for encouraging me to write this story. As much as I hate to admit, so much of this is based on true events.

CHAPTER ONE

Gum. Just my luck. I found the one spot in an empty parking lot where somebody spit out a piece of gum and I stepped right into it. The sticky pink glob spread beneath my heel and I grimaced in disgust. I leaned against the car to scrape it off, but lost my balance and stepped in it again with my other heel. Not just any heels, but my Jimmy Choos.

"Are you fucking kidding me?" I asked no one. Both shoes were covered with tiny strings of gum and I was almost late to my meeting with my boss, Erin Waters. I shuffled over the asphalt to scuff more off on my way into the building. Not a great way to start my morning. I already knew shit was going to hit the fan because Erin rarely asked for a meeting. I gave up on the gum knowing I'd much rather deal with it later than worry about a disgruntled boss. I pulled at the front door a few times before I remembered it was a push through door. Lynn, the receptionist at *Mainstream*, saw me and laughed. As I'm sure she did everyone who fell victim to the backward door.

"Good morning, Kennedy. Nice to see you again." Waters Publishing did a great thing when they hired her. She was the friendliest, and most helpful, receptionist.

"Lynn, please tell me you didn't see me out there in the parking lot."

"No. I did not see you zombie walk in the parking lot and wonder why. Not at all." She winked at me. I groaned.

"Hopefully you're the only one who did." I wanted to sit and chat with her, but I was expected upstairs. "Wish me luck." I caught the elevator to the fifth floor and quickened my step the closer I got to Erin's office. The door was slightly ajar so I busted in. She was expecting me.

"Good morning, Kennedy. Have a seat. Would you like some coffee or a doughnut?" Her nicety threw me off. The tiny hairs on the back of my neck stood at attention. Something was up.

"Why are you being nice to me?" The wolf-like grin on my boss's face wasn't the endearing kind of smile. My stomach sank. "Oh, hell. What do you want me to do?"

"It's not that bad. I need you to cover a story for *A&A's* August issue. You know I have to hold my brother's hand during the transition, so I need to make sure he succeeds. His success starts with me and ends with you." Travis had just graduated with his Master's degree and their family was grooming him to take over *Antlers & Anglers*, Waters Publishing's magazine focused on anything to do with the great outdoors.

I stared at Erin for a long time. She broke eye contact first. "You're not serious, are you? Look at me. I'm cut out for city life. Besides, I'm almost certain I'm allergic to nature and bugs." Erin pretended to ignore me and scribbled something on her notepad. The silence dragged. "Come on, Erin. I've paid my dues."

We didn't talk about what happened six months ago when Nikki Toles, soccer player extraordinaire, ruined my professional life. At least, we didn't talk about it anymore.

It was supposed to be a simple interview. *Mainstream* had several journalists on staff who specialized in celebrity interviews, but I was the best and Erin wanted Nikki on the cover. After Nikki's team won the national championship title, I scheduled an interview with the Most Valuable Player. It started off innocently enough. Dinner, laughter, a few drinks at the hotel bar. We took the interview to her room because we were constantly getting interrupted by her fans downstairs.

The interview stopped the minute Nikki stripped down and straddled my lap. The sex was intense, furious, and the things she did to me would still be delightful if the nasty lawsuit her husband slapped on Waters Publishing didn't prevent me from enjoying the memories. I hadn't realized their marriage was still a thing. She had assured me it was over, but he thought differently. I cooperated and supplied our lawyers with the text messages and emails Nikki sent me. Through the grapevine, I found out I was not her first indiscretion and I doubted I'd be the last. I hadn't heard from her since the lawsuit.

Erin yanked me from my dream job of hanging out and interviewing the rich and famous as a form of punishment for not being professional. For the last six months, I'd written boring articles on old celebrities that people had forgotten about, and written several where-are-they-now pieces about fifteen minutes of fame internet stars. I missed my old life and felt it slipping away more and more with every ridiculous story I reported. But this was the first time she threw me the nature curve.

"I understand this isn't something you normally cover, but you are one of my best writers and you can make it sound sexy and appealing. Plus, it will put a new spin on an otherwise boring story to tell it through the eyes of someone who never goes fishing."

"That's not enough of a reason to send me on an *A&A* story. It doesn't make any sense," I said.

Erin nodded. "Here's the kicker. I'm glad you're sitting down. Dustin Collings agreed to do an interview. He somehow managed to get a reality show about deep-sea fishing."

"Oh, fuck. Not him." Dustin was the biggest asshole on reality television. He got kicked off of the show *Survive This* and somehow managed to stay afloat by bouncing from low budget reality shows to creepy late night commercials. I thought long and hard before I answered Erin. "No." I couldn't believe I told her no after everything we'd been through. The look on her face informed me that wasn't an option. "I mean, there has to be someone better qualified. I'm sure Jacob or Brian would love to go fishing and write about this dude. Why don't you pick either one of them?"

"Because I want you to go. Celebrity interviews sell magazines and you're the best at celebrity interviews. This is huge for *A&A*." I sighed and opened my mouth to protest again, but she cut me off before I squeaked out another word. "Plus, Travis is doing an overhaul of his staff. He doesn't have anyone capable of doing a feature." I tried to cut in, but Erin kept talking. "I'll tell you what. You do this one thing, and I'll put you back on A-list interviews with *Mainstream* full-time. You get to go back to the cream of the crop and the lifestyle you love. Do we have a deal?"

"I want that in writing this time," I said. She smiled and started typing on her computer. In a minute, she had a simple two sentence agreement. She signed, then handed it to me. I added my signature, and handed it back. She buzzed her assistant, Gabrielle, to make a copy of it for me. It wasn't legally binding, but I knew it was enough to get Erin to keep her word. I smiled for the first time all morning. "Where am I going? Channel Islands? San Diego? Baja?" I wracked my brain and listed off all of the ocean fishing near LA.

"Anchorage, Alaska," Erin said.

"Are you fucking kidding me?" It was the second time I'd asked that question in ten minutes. "I'm not prepared to go someplace so rustic." My mind automatically raced through my closet. I had heels, dresses, and skirts. My sweaters were cashmere and definitely more fashionable than practical.

"Go to Accounting and grab a per diem check. Spend some of that on a pair of boots and a few thick soccer mom sweatshirts. I doubt Alaska at the end of April is parka weather. And take a camera. I'll need photos, too." It was almost as if Erin read my mind. My panic was evident.

"How long am I supposed to be there?"

"Until you get the story. It's the feature. We need to have it written, edited, and sent to press in six weeks. Four would be better.

Go there and figure out the angle." She pretended to cast a line and then laughed at her fishing pun. I rolled my eyes. "Seriously, find something new and exciting with this guy and deep-sea fishing. So much has been written about it already. I'm hoping that somebody who doesn't have the experience can find a refreshing side. Travis scored a ton of Alaskan adventure advertisements for the August release, so I thought it would be a good idea to make Alaska the magazine's feature story. We trust you. Just get it done and do it well." She dismissed me and I sulked all the way to her office door.

"When do you want me to leave?"

"Are you still here?"

CHAPTER TWO

R ight away I noticed two things about Anchorage. First, the airport was ridiculously tiny compared to LAX, and second, the Alaskan mountains were the most majestic I'd ever seen. Giant, massive white peaks that stopped me in my tracks when I stepped off of the plane. The mountains in California were gorgeous, but I was more of a coastal girl and spent my vacations at the beach. The last time I was on a snowcapped mountaintop was fifteen years ago on a high school ski trip to Big Bear.

Since I slept on the plane and had to be poked awake by a flight attendant, I missed our descent and the view from above. I wanted to take pictures of my first introduction to the ranges, but I refrained. I had at least three weeks to get better pictures than what I could standing on an airport tarmac. My main focus was learning all I could about fishing before I had my interview with Dustin Collings. If I didn't have at least the basics down, he was the kind of man who would viciously tear me apart if I said the wrong word.

I secured a luxury sedan at the car rental place that was about two steps away from the ticket counter. How was this place so small? They offered me an SUV, but I hadn't driven anything bigger than my convertible Volkswagen Beetle in years so I stuck with simple and practical. And expensive. I was amazed they had a Lexus as a rental option in the middle of nowhere.

Feeling refreshed after my five-hour nap, I decided to drive around before finding a place to land. How busy could Anchorage be this time of year? It was what they considered 'off season' so I expected I could grab a room just about anywhere. Besides, I wanted to check out the hotels before I gave them my credit card information.

My stomach rumbled, reminding me that I hadn't eaten since the night before. I needed to find some food and fast. I recognized a few chain restaurants, none of which offered a decent salad. Most restaurants were local so I picked the nicest looking one and parked. I shivered as I stepped out of the car. The weather was chillier than I expected. Since my warm clothes were limited, I'd traveled wearing a pair of slacks, a blouse, a thin, yet fashionable sweater that brought out the copper color in my brown eyes, and sensible heels. I hadn't been able to bring myself to wear the clothes I'd bought with my per diem check. The two thick sweaters, two sweatshirts, two pairs of fashionable jeans, jacket, and hiking boots were packed in my suitcase. It had been hard to find warm clothes in Los Angeles, especially with only a day's notice. All of the stores were racks of summer clothes only. As a result, none of my purchases were up to my usual standard.

A tiny bell dinged above me when I pushed through the diner's door. The announcing bell was unnecessary as every single person in the joint stopped eating and stared at me. Either Anchorage didn't get a lot of tourists, or I looked like a mess. I subconsciously patted down my hair and smoothed out my sweater. Did I have sleep lines on my face? Was something stuck in my hair? A fast moving waitress pointed to a booth near the back of the restaurant.

"Grab a seat there. I'll be with you in a moment." I walked past everybody in the restaurant with confidence I lacked and slid into the back booth. The bustling waitress threw a cup of coffee in front of me and handed me a menu.

"I just want water to drink, thanks," I said. I picked up the menu and hoped for something healthy. The waitress didn't leave, apparently wanting my decision right then. I ordered a garden salad with oil and vinegar on the side. She rolled her eyes at me.

"Are you sure you don't want some chicken or mashed potatoes? Our meatloaf special's very popular." I shook my head and handed her back the menu. She nodded at me and zipped away, leaving the cup of coffee.

I pulled out my phone, checked my emails, and informed Erin I'd made it to Alaska without a hitch. As much as I wanted a copy of the daily newspaper located just to the left of the cash register, I wasn't going to parade myself in front of these people again. One look over was enough for me. I was used to a certain type of attention and this wasn't the kind I liked. I immediately felt like an outsider. I should've changed my clothes right away. I stuck out like a sore thumb. Most people were in sweatshirts, jeans, and boots.

My waitress returned and slid a glass of water with only a few tiny ice cubes floating on top in front of me. No lemon. I wasn't about to ask her for it either. I tried connecting with her by flashing her my award winning smile, but she ignored me and hurried back to the kitchen. The coffee was still on the table. She returned a moment later. Her name tag said Nita. I wondered if it was short for anything, but I didn't dare ask.

"One garden salad, dressing on the side." The wooden bowl it was served in rattled and clanked as she all but dropped it in front of me. I was almost afraid to ask for silverware, but she pulled out a set from her apron pocket and slid it my way. "Do you need anything else?"

Nope. I shook my head and she buzzed off to grab another pot of coffee from the burner. Coffee was obviously a thing here.

I spent my lunch people watching and nibbling on lettuce. Even though it was noon, the environment was laid back. Nobody was in a hurry, so unlike Los Angeles. I waved off the offer for pie. I couldn't remember the last time I ate a pastry. I counted every calorie and every gram of sugar. I hadn't cheated on my diet in years. I'd convinced myself that smelling baked goods was just as satisfying as eating them. I was too thin, but my environment was a competitive one and I had to stay in shape and thin to fit in.

Nita picked up my empty bowl. "Wow. Where did you put all of that greenery?" She was either trying to be funny, or rude. I honestly couldn't tell. She slapped the bill on my table and left before I responded. The salad was eight ninety-five, the water was free, and the coffee I didn't touch was a dollar ninety-nine. I sighed. It wasn't worth the fight. I slid a three-dollar tip under the saltshaker and made my way to the cash register.

"Where are you from?" The cashier didn't even try to be subtle. At least she smiled at me.

"California. I'm here doing a story on fishing." She snorted and covered it up with a cough. Apparently I wasn't the first one to ever write a story on it. "I need to do some research before I start my interview. Any advice on who to talk to around here?" She handed me several different brochures from underneath the counter.

"This should get you started. There are several different kinds of fishing. Obviously salmon's the most popular around here. If you head south on AK-1, you'll hit Homer. That's the place for halibut. I guess it all depends on what type of fishing you are looking to cover." I grabbed my receipt and thanked her for her help. I got more out of her in thirty seconds than I did out of Nita in forty minutes. According to one of the tiny maps, there were only five major highways in Alaska. I couldn't get lost.

With a full stomach and renewed ambition, I decided to go on an adventure. I was anxious to get out of town and get closer to the mountains. People fished straight off of the highways and were clearly visible from the road. At least that's what the brochure showed. I was sure to find somebody who was willing to talk to me. Not everybody was going to be like Nita. I had faith. I was going to know so much about fishing, Dustin Collings wasn't going to know what hit him.

CHAPTER THREE

I was completely lost. I stopped at a T in the road and waited. It had been almost twenty minutes since I saw another car on this stretch of highway. I was positive that as long as I stuck to one of the five main highways, I couldn't get lost. At least the scenery was breathtaking. Grandiose didn't even begin to describe the different ranges. I rolled down my window and breathed in the clean, crisp afternoon air. A thin fog grazed the tips of the firs and created a quiet, eerie ambiance that upon further thought, didn't make me entirely comfortable. It was too quiet. Suddenly, I felt alone and scared for the first time in a long time. I'd been driving a few hours and made the mistake of daringly turning on a road to reach a lake I could see off in the distance. At least my gas tank was half-full. I checked my maps app. Even it didn't know where I was.

I heard a noise from across the street. Naturally, my mind conjured up several horrible possible scenarios. An axe murderer swinging his axe through the underbrush to clear a path to me. Or maybe it was a mountain man who hadn't seen a woman in years. I quickly rolled up my windows and locked my doors several times as if the first click didn't actually lock them. I laughed and sighed with relief when the mysterious noisemaker was a moose with her calf pressed closely to her side. I turned in my seat to reach into my luggage for the camera. When I twisted back around, I was not prepared to be eye to eye with the big moose. I yelped and accidentally honked my horn.

I regretted it immediately. Instead of scaring the moose away, the mama moose went into wild beast mode and leaned her giant, furry body against the Lexus, jarring it. I screamed as true panic set in. I couldn't even put the car in reverse because the baby, who was actually the size of a small horse, was behind me. Even though I feared for my life, I didn't want to go down in history as the tourist who purposely killed a baby moose. The mother slid her body up the front of the car and plopped her rear end down on the left side of the hood. I watched in horror as the hood crushed the engine. I didn't know what was worse—the deep, gurgling sounds of the pissed off moose, or the expensive metal twisting into itself. It was a car wreck in super slow motion. I furiously scrambled from the front seat to the middle of the back seat. I didn't want to die this way.

"Go away! Get out of here." I didn't sound brave even to myself. The moose was half sitting on my car and didn't show any signs of moving. I grabbed my phone from the cup holder and called 9-1-1. The signal was sketchy and weak, but I got an operator. "Hello? Yes. Hello? There's a moose on my car."

"What happened exactly? How did you agitate the moose to prompt it to sit on your car?" The operator did not sound concerned about my well-being, which pissed me off.

"I didn't agitate it at all. I was parked on the road and it just came up to me," I said.

"Moose don't just sit on cars, ma'am."

I shook my head and listened to the operator blame me for the attack. "Well, this one did. Does it matter why? I need help."

He sighed. "All right. We will send someone to your location. Where are you?"

"I have no idea. I don't know the street I'm on, but I think I made it back to Highway 1. Some idiot took the sign off of the post. The last town I remember was Alyeska or something like that, I think. Okay, now the baby's circling the car."

"There's also a baby?" he asked.

"Yes, there's a baby moose here, too."

"Why didn't you mention that previously? That's a problem."

"What do you mean 'that's a problem'?" I clutched the phone closer to my ear and sank lower in the back seat. Up close and personal, the calf I thought was adorable was actually foaming at the mouth. Did moose have rabies? A Jeep approached from down the road. "Wait. I see a car. And it's slowing down." I waved my hands as if a moose sitting on my car wasn't going to attract enough attention for somebody to at least stop and hopefully help. "I'll call you back." I placed all of my faith in a sandy brown Jeep Grand Cherokee. I almost wept when I read Alaskan Wildlife Rescue on the side. The person parked in the middle of the road, in front of my car. There was enough of a gap, though, between it and the moose. A woman leaned out and waved her arms at the moose on my car.

"Let's go, Martha. You and Tuffy go home." She turned on her red and blue lights to distract the moose, but perturbed, destructive Martha didn't budge. When the woman shrilled a siren in three short bursts, Martha begrudgingly stood up, groaned at either me or Tuffy, and moseyed down the street as if the last ten minutes didn't just happen.

I didn't move until the moose were no longer visible. I closed my eyes and willed my heart to slow down. A knock on my window startled me and I opened my eyes to see a very tall and very attractive woman looking at me. Concern was etched on her face and her big, gray eyes seemed trustworthy. I felt safe.

"Are you all right?" She pointed to the handle. "Unlock your door."

I was squished down in the seat and had to reach to unlock it. I took a deep breath before I responded. The woman squatted so that we were eye to eye. Her forest green uniform fit her perfectly and it was hard not to stare. The name Coleman was patched right above her right breast. She was butch all the way down to her shiny black boots. My rapid heartbeat switched from fear to excitement when our eyes met again. Her jet-black hair, short on the sides, long on top, fell forward across her forehead. She ran her fingers through it and brushed it back out of her face.

"Thank you." That's all I said. She was gorgeous and tall. Two of my favorite traits. Due to recent harrowing events, my game was off so I gave up on flirting. For the moment.

"You're welcome. I'm Brynn. Brynn Coleman." Her smile was endearing and I found myself returning the smile even though I'd just experienced a pretty shitty encounter with nature.

"I'm Kennedy Wells. I'm completely lost and did absolutely nothing to provoke that moose. I honestly don't even know what just happened."

"I believe you," she said.

I snorted, recalling how the 9-1-1 operator had a different opinion.

"Moose are temperamental, especially where babies are concerned. How are you? Are you hurt anywhere?" I shook my head and inched my way, not very gracefully, over to the door. I grabbed my heels that fell off during the struggle to get from the front seat to the back and tossed them on the ground before I stepped out of the car. Brynn hitched her eyebrow when she looked at my shoes. "You aren't from around here, are you?"

Heat blossomed over my cheeks. I should've changed my clothes when I first landed, but I planned on an easy first day. The goal was to drive around and get to know a few popular fishing holes or streams, then set up shop at a hotel in town. It didn't go as planned. Worst first day on assignment ever.

"No. I'm from Los Angeles. I'm lost and my rental car's completely destroyed. I just got here. My boss is going to kill me." I shook as the adrenaline left my body.

"Do you have a jacket you can put on?"

"I'm not cold. I just think this is me coming down from a brush with death."

"Well, the weather changes quickly this time of year and a jacket might make you feel better," she said.

I unzipped one of my bags and pulled out a fleece jacket that didn't match my outfit, but warmed me nicely. Brynn looked me up and down. Her stare landed at my footwear. "I know, I know. I'm completely ill prepared for Alaska." I tilted my head back to look at her. God, she was so tall and I felt the butterflies stir as my attraction grew. She was at least six feet in those boots. "Is there anyone you can suggest to get my car towed? I can't imagine it's drivable." Brynn walked over to the side of my car to investigate. I followed her because I didn't want to be alone and her presence made me safe. She pulled on the fender scrunched into the tire. It didn't budge. The dent in the hood was so deep that the sides bent upward like a bird in flight. "Does this happen a lot in Alaska? Innocent people getting attacked by moose?"

She turned to face me and rested her hip against the beat up fender. "Like most animals, they are pretty protective of their young. Martha felt threatened by you. Did you do anything to provoke her?" Her, too? She sounded just like the 9-1-1 operator. I rolled my eyes, but before I spouted out a sarcastic response, she gave me a list of possibilities. "Did you get out of the car to take pictures of them? Did you rev the engine by mistake or honk the horn?" Guilty. I backed down immediately.

"I did honk the horn, but that was an accident because she scared me. I was parked right here. I didn't move the car or anything." I sounded whiny.

"They don't like loud noises. Moose will charge, whereas other animals like brown bears will usually leave if you make a lot of noise. You just had a run in with the wrong animal."

"So you are telling me it's better to cross paths with a bear than a moose?"

"It's just better to not have a run in with any wildlife." She folded her arms across her chest and stared at me. I shivered at her intensity. "If you're going to be here in Alaska a while, I suggest you stick to the towns and main roads. Well, when you get your new rental car." There was a hint of a smile on her face, which angered me because while I found it annoying, it also heightened her attractiveness. "I can call one of our rangers to come and tow your car back to town. Where are you staying?"

"I don't have any place yet. I was just driving around, getting a feel for Alaska before I searched out a hotel. I think I'm going to stick with Anchorage. More people, fewer animals."

"Right now we're about thirty miles from Anchorage." She walked confidently back to her Jeep and leaned into the window to reach her radio. I got a great view of her tight uniform and even though it wasn't polite to look, I stole a few extra seconds to appreciate her form. I took a step back when she approached me again. "If you feel comfortable, you can stay here, inside the car, and wait for Rick. He'll be here in thirty minutes. Or, if you prefer, I'm on my way to a rescue and after I'm done, I can drop you off wherever you want. You can spend the time calling the rental place, or your boss, or husband."

I didn't hesitate. "I'll go with you. I don't want to stay out here any longer than necessary. Can I bring my stuff or should I leave it?"

She leaned down to look into the back seat. Even though I knew what I had back there, I looked, too. Two suitcases, a camera bag, and a small carry-on that included my laptop and some essential items. When she turned to give me her answer, her lips barely brushed my ear. I felt her warm breath on the side of my neck and chills raced along my arms. Surprise registered in her eyes. I watched as they darted down to my mouth, then back to my eyes. Her tongue shot out to quickly lick her lips. She didn't move. Neither did I. Well, well, well. I was even more interested in Brynn Coleman after she unknowingly gave me the information I wanted.

"Um. Sure. They'll fit. Let me pull the Jeep around and we can transfer your luggage." She stepped away from me quickly and turned on her heel.

"Should I push my car over onto the shoulder more?"

Her laugh echoed around us. "No. You won't have to worry about causing a traffic jam here. Ranger Rick will probably be the next person on this road." She whipped the Jeep around and parked next to me.

I stood back as she scooped my luggage and arranged them in her back seat. "Thank you for coming to my rescue. I do appreciate it." I placed my keys on the top of the back tire for Rick, per her request.

A blush crept across her face. "It's no problem. I'm just glad you're okay. I'm sorry about your car though." She climbed in the Jeep and waited until I buckled up. "Feel free to make all the calls you need to. We have a twenty minute drive ahead of us." I watched her out of the corner of my eye. How old was she? She looked younger than me, but her confidence made me think she was around my age, early thirties. No ring, no jewelry at all, not even earrings. I had so many bracelets on that the animals heard me coming a mile away. Her skin looked soft and touchable. And that hair. It was sexy and messy. She was the kind of woman who woke up looking that good. What was she doing all the way up here in Alaska?

CHAPTER FOUR

"Wait a minute. Do you really have a Ranger Rick?" We'd been driving in silence for a few minutes and I couldn't stand the quiet any longer.

Brynn laughed. "He hates it when we call him that, so naturally, the whole office does."

"What do you do?" I asked.

"I'm a park ranger and the director of the Alaskan Wildlife Rescue and Sanctuary outside of Anchorage. We answer calls about animals in distress or in difficult situations and try to help them out the best we can. I'm on my way to assess an owl that a local, Mrs. Wright, called about. She thinks some coyotes got ahold of it and it can't fly." Brynn was quick to explain further when she saw the horrified look on my face. "If he can't fly, I'll bring him back to the shelter and one of our veterinarians will take a look at him. We're good about patching animals up and setting them free. If we don't think they will make it out there, we keep them at Spa Sanctuary."

I felt a little bit better. I took the remaining time to call the rental place and let them know what happened and what to expect when Rick arrived with the car. I breathed a heavy sigh of relief because I agreed to their additional insurance. They promised me everything was fine, but were obviously annoyed. They guaranteed me an SUV when they got the car back. Of course, I'd have to fill out a ton of paperwork first.

Brynn slowed the Jeep and turned right onto a dirt road that wasn't visible from the highway. I was positive she didn't just kidnap me. Almost positive. We drove through mounds of tall dead brown weeds that bowed from recent snow until we saw an opening ahead. As we drove up the hill, a log cabin appeared. It leaned a bit too far to the left and had a roof that should have been replaced years ago. Mrs. Wright, I presumed, was standing outside with a gun on her hip and a cigarette clasped between her forefinger and middle finger. She pointed her cigarette over at the barn.

"Brynn. He's over there somewhere. The coyotes are getting braver." Brynn directed the Jeep over to the barn and slowed her speed.

"We don't want to scare him any more than he already is." Brynn spotted him by the barn and parked the car. "He's not full grown yet. He's panicked and doesn't know what to do. I'll have to be discreet and slow." She put her finger to her lips signaling me to be quiet.

I looked at her full, red lips and wondered if they were as soft as they looked. When my eyes met hers again, they widened in surprise. Perhaps I wasn't as inconspicuous with my lustful look as I thought. I nodded that I understood. She carefully opened the back of the Jeep and unlatched the door to a cage that filled the entire cargo area.

"It's okay, baby. I'm not going to hurt you." Even though she was talking to an injured animal, her soothing voice was quite sexy.

The white and dark spotted owl panted heavily, but finally stopped squawking. I was nervous because Mrs. Wright mentioned coyotes and I didn't know where they were. My overactive imagination had them tearing through the dead weeds right for Brynn and the crippled owl. Crawling on her hands and knees, she swiftly closed the distance and carefully tossed a piece of material over it.

"Is he going to be okay?" I asked after she had him secured in the cage. "That was amazing, by the way." Why I didn't think to take pictures of the rescue was beyond me.

"I don't think his wing's broken. I didn't feel anything out of place and he bent it back okay for a few seconds. It might just be sprained. Maybe he hit the side of the barn and knocked himself out. If he were full grown, it would have turned out differently."

"That's a baby? He's huge." I turned around to look past my luggage to see him, but I could only see the top of his bobbing head and a few white fuzzy feathers of his outstretched wing. Brynn called the sanctuary to let them know we would be there in about fifteen minutes.

"He's more of a teenager. Once he gets to be an adult, he will be completely white and his wing span will be somewhere between four and five feet."

"I'm amazed he's out today. Aren't owls usually nocturnal?"

"The snow owl hunts twenty four hours a day. They don't care if it's light or dark out. Most of the snow owls are in northern Alaska so this guy's quite a treat."

"You learn something new every day. How long have you been doing this? Helping animals out, I mean. Was it always your dream job? Am I asking too many questions?" I got into journalism to satisfy my over-the-top curiosity.

"It's my dream job now," she said. She offered no other explanation and I didn't push her.

"I'm working my way back to my dream job," I said.

"What is it you do exactly?" She turned to look at me and again she looked at my lips.

"I'm a writer for *Mainstream* magazine." I waited for that to sink in. Brynn couldn't have cared less. I'd have to impress her a different way.

"But you're here for work, right?" The question in her voice was more accusatory than I would have liked.

"I'm writing a story about a reality star who scored a fishing show here."

Brynn rolled her eyes. Apparently she knew about Dustin. "Yeah, Anchorage has seen more visitors than normal before fishing season this year. I heard rumors about a new show stationed from here."

"I normally write about celebrities, but I'm kind of on probation and my boss stuck me with this fishing story that unfortunately involves him. That's why I'm here. She didn't give me much of a choice. Honestly, I know exactly zero about fishing. Or nature."

Brynn suppressed a smile. "I'm sure your boss knows you're good or else why would she send you here? To fail? That's just money out of her pocket."

"Um. Thank you? I think."

Brynn laughed. "You're welcome and yes, that was a compliment. Sometimes it's better to have fresh eyes. So your magazine is equivalent to *People* or *Entertainment?*"

I gave her a nod mixed with a frown. "Basically, yes. I like to think we focus on more than just the normal celebrity gossip. Sure, we might bring up whatever's going on with that person, but we try to get the human interest behind their decisions. And we don't drop it and move on to the next new hot button."

"It sounds like you take it pretty seriously."

"I do. People tend to write off celebrity reporting, but I like the contacts I've made and I love it when a celebrity trusts me enough to call me with news or give me the big break."

"Oh, so you are kind of a celebrity, too." She slowed to make a turn. We were probably getting close to the sanctuary.

"Not at all," I said. I loved the attention, for sure. My list of contacts in my phone included several actors, musicians, and sports players. It took me years to assemble my list. In a superficial way, I was proud, but I didn't think Brynn cared so I downplayed my success. "It's just what I do. I'm one of the lucky ones who loves her job." Brynn nodded but didn't say anything. We rounded another corner and once we cleared the trees, I gasped. The sanctuary was set at the base of a mountain range. The visitor center was a massive log cabin with large floor to ceiling windows. Several smaller buildings were visible in the distance, all linked by boardwalks which I assumed protected a delicate ecosystem below. "Wow. This place is huge. And what a fantastic view. Wait a minute. Is that a bear?"

"That's Yogi. Melissa's in there, too. We rescued them when they were cubs. Let me get this owl to Tina and then if you want, I can show you around a bit. I mean, if you have time. I know you have a lot going on."

I smiled at her nervousness. "I'd love that. I think I can spare a few minutes. I mean, this is part of nature. I'm sure to learn something."

She flashed me a quick smile and headed inside with the cage. I didn't venture far from the Jeep. I was unsure of the property and didn't want to end up a punching bag for Yogi or Melissa because I wandered into the wrong area. I saw *The Revenant* and that movie scared the shit out of me. Now that I knew moose were just as dangerous, I decided I should do most of my reporting from inside city limits. Any city. I headed over to the information sign to read more about the sanctuary and rescue. It was a huge operation with hundreds of acres dedicated to providing the best home for all kinds of animals who could no longer survive out in the wilderness for one reason or another. Injuries were the most common reason. I had a thousand questions for Brynn when she returned. I looked at the time. There was no way I'd be able to ask all my questions that afternoon.

"Sorry about that. I had to help Tina get our little friend out of the cage. He didn't want to cooperate the minute I put the cage on the table," Brynn said from behind me.

I turned. Everything about her took my breath away. Maybe it was because she was so different from the women I dated. Most were femme, had long hair, wore tons of make-up, and wore short, summer dresses. Brynn was the polar opposite. Or maybe it was just the sure, authoritative way she carried herself wearing that tight uniform.

"I've been thinking. I would like to spend more time here this week, but I'm kind of stressed today. I'm afraid that the car rental place might close soon. Can you please take me into town and once I get settled, I can come back out here?" That sounded self-absorbed, but there wasn't any other way around it.

"That's fine. I grabbed a few local maps of streams and lakes and highlighted a few that are popular. It's not fishing season here in Anchorage yet, but there are several commercial fishermen who work year round that you could talk to." She handed me the flyers and I smiled at her thoughtfulness.

"Thank you. Are there any good hotels in town that you can recommend?" I felt like I was using her kindness. I should've done a better job preparing for this trip, but Erin didn't give me enough time. "And to thank you for all of your help, I would love to take you to lunch or dinner sometime this week when you have time." I figured the invitation softened my neediness.

"You don't need to, Kennedy. I don't mind helping out. Plus, this makes for a good story I can tell the other rangers during our potluck dinner next week." She winked at me as she pulled out of the parking lot.

I cringed. "It's a horrible story. I hate that I have to tell my boss. She loves ammunition on me. That's what got me into this mess in the first place." I didn't elaborate and Brynn didn't ask. "Not mess, but predicament." I corrected myself.

"As far as a place to stay for a few weeks, we do have nice hotels, but I think in order for you to really appreciate Alaska, you should rent a cabin. They can be cheaper than a hotel and I could get you a good deal on a nice one. My friend owns several not too far from here. Well-stocked, comfortable, and hopefully inspirational. It's easy driving distance to the wharf so you won't have trouble with your interview," she said.

"That sounds like a good plan. Thank you again." I owed this woman everything. I couldn't imagine anyone being this nice to me back home without wanting something in return.

"The cabins are on our way. Less than ten minutes. We can swing in, and if you hate them, I can recommend the Crowne Plaza, or the Homewood Suites in the heart of downtown," she said.

We arrived in eight minutes and I was immediately taken with the view. The front of the cabins faced a crystal clear lake with snowcapped mountains off in the near distance. Behind the cabins sat the city. I felt safe with society only a few miles away. This location was ideal.

"I love this place."

"Let me go check with Cee and find out availability," Brynn said. She disappeared into the large cabin that was obviously the office. Two large dogs escaped when she opened the door and galloped straight for me. I took a few steps backward, unsure of their intentions. A sharp whistle pierced the air and both dogs stopped in their tracks. A tiny dachshund came out of nowhere and pushed her way past the two big dogs to jump up against my legs. The welcoming committee was on point. The three faces staring at me made me want to pet them.

Brynn peeked back out the door to make sure I was okay. "Meet Murphy and King. They are sweet. You can pet them."

I stretched my hand out to let them sniff me. The dachshund danced in front of me on her hind legs, begging me to pet her. I wasn't about to kneel and rub her belly when she flopped on her back though. I had no idea what the other two dogs would do. They seemed nice, but so did Stephen King's Cujo. One of the dogs actually looked like him. He was a St. Bernard mix. The other was a chocolate lab with a pink nose. After they confirmed I was not a threat, they headed over to the Jeep to sniff around the back of it. I was sure the injured owl's scent was still strong.

"Kennedy," Brynn called. I made my way to the porch, avoiding the little dachshund dancing around my feet. She was bound and determined to be my friend. "I see you've met Heidi. She's kind of a lover." I was afraid that I would step on her, but she was fast and didn't get underfoot. "I have keys to a cabin just over there. Want to go check it out?"

I nodded and followed Brynn along the dirt path. "There doesn't seem to be anybody around." I noticed most of the cabins were unoccupied.

"Well, you are here before the tourism and fishing seasons officially start. That's why we're looking at the big cabin because it's available and I think you will like it. There's parking right next to it. There's a grill out front, but don't forget to clean it off if you use it. You don't want another animal problem." Brynn unlocked the door and flipped on the lights. She stepped back and waited for me to slip past her to take a look around.

"This place is gorgeous. Is the bedroom there?" I pointed to the loft and decided that even if it wasn't, I was going to sleep there. There were so many windows and I pictured myself falling asleep while staring at the stars.

"Yes. You still might be able to see the northern lights from there. They are usually not visible this late in spring, but they might make an appearance. There's also a second bedroom over there, a kitchenette, and a fireplace. The only thing you don't have here is room service. There's a coffee maker, though. And I believe Cee puts out coffee cake and fruit every morning in the office cabin," Brynn said. She blew right by the part about the northern lights as if everybody on the planet experienced them all of the time.

I was excited about the cabin and had to refrain from bouncing up and down on the balls of my feet like an eager eight-year-old. "How much does she want a night?"

"Well, she rents it by the week which will work out for you. She can give you a steep discount for the next two weeks, then it will jump to seasonal rates if you stay past that." Brynn handed me an invoice. My jaw dropped opened at the amount. It was a steal. Brynn was doing me a favor.

"Sold. Or yes. Whatever. Definitely. Where do I sign?"

"Let's head back to the main cabin and you can meet Cee. We can unload the Jeep so you only have to worry about a new car and not your stuff. Ranger Rick already dropped it off so you shouldn't have a problem getting one that hasn't been destroyed. Yet," she said. She did a great job of not smiling when she delivered that punch.

"The car's already there? Thank you so much. I think meeting you was the best thing that's happened to me. I'm definitely taking you to dinner this week. You pick the date and time and I'll treat," I said.

She blushed and stammered. Brynn was confident in everything except women. And maybe I read her wrong, but I was sure she played on my team. She was dapper, handsome, and gave me chills. I'd never been wrong about a woman. I stayed clear of the straight ones except for friendship, and enjoyed myself physically with women who liked women. I hadn't had time for a relationship in years. The occasional hookup was inevitable when self-gratification was boring, but it never led to anything but a quick lay. Nobody in Los Angeles or Hollywood was exclusive it seemed. I wasn't going to try either.

"Remind me to give you one of my business cards before I drop you off," Brynn said.

We headed to the main cabin so I could leave my credit card information and meet Cee. Even if Brynn forgot to give me her contact information, I knew I could reach her through Cee. It was an easier way that didn't involve me lost on a deserted stretch of the Alaskan highway alone with a family of disgruntled moose.

• 41 •

CHAPTER FIVE

I decided to hang around Anchorage and do old-fashioned research at the public library. Plus the library's internet wasn't spotty like the reception at the cabins. The day before had been a disaster and I wanted at least one day that didn't destroy my spirits. I was banking on today. I called Dustin Collings to nail down the details of our interview, but was forced to leave a message. I wasn't upset about it. I didn't want to admit that he could make my day worse, but he probably would have. After eating some fruit and yogurt, I headed to the closest library and settled in for the day. I was one of two patrons there so I didn't feel like I needed to be quiet.

The librarian, Mandy, was an attractive woman who was probably ten years older than me. With her dark eyes, long dark hair, and high cheekbones, I guessed she was Inuit. She was extremely helpful in getting information that couldn't be found on the internet. It was dated, but I was able to pull out a few nuggets of data that further educated me on deep-sea fishing—the fun, the rewards, and the perils of it. She showed me old fishing maps, framed photos of some of the largest fish I'd ever seen, and a few trinkets fishermen discovered inside fish they caught. The stories she told me were fascinating, yet nothing I could document other than as local folklore. That was a fun angle to think about. Details like that helped make stories come alive.

Fishing around Anchorage wasn't a thing until mid-May. That deflated my inspiration. My interview with Dustin wasn't for a few more days so I had to occupy my time getting into the spirit of the story. Mandy informed me that other Alaskan cities started fishing in April, but they were quite the drive from Anchorage. Today wasn't the day I was going to drive. I was still getting used to the size of the SUV the car rental place gave me. I had to ask for the extra coverage because for the first time ever, they didn't push. I already had a reputation with them.

"Don't forget to take some time to drive around Alaska just to soak in the beauty," Mandy said.

I snorted and nodded. She quirked her eyebrow at me. I was too embarrassed to tell her my story, so instead, I thanked her for her help and sat back down at my table.

She interrupted me after a few hours to suggest a few local restaurants for lunch. "If you are going to write a story about fishing, maybe you should taste the different kinds. Lucille's across the street serves great halibut. It's their lunch special today." I looked up from a diary I was reading about an explorer who traipsed across Alaska in the early eighteen hundreds. There was nothing helpful for me, but the story was so interesting, I lost track of time.

"That's a great idea." I gathered my stack of books to return them before leaving for lunch, but Mandy waved me off.

"You can just leave them there. Nobody will disturb them," she said.

"Do you want to come with me? It would be great to talk to somebody from here." If anyone could tell me great stories, I figured it would be the local librarian.

"Sure. Let me just tell my clerk that I'm leaving for a bit." I watched her walk away and wondered what the LGBT population was like in Alaska. I got the lesbian vibe from her like I did Brynn. She grabbed her coat and we walked over to Lucille's. The waitress seated us right away, even though there was a wait. Nobody cared that we cut in front of the line. Maybe Mandy was kind of a big deal here.

"How did you manage that? Not a single person complained. I'm from Los Angeles. If we tried that there, every single person would bitch," I said.

"My mom's Lucille. And nobody messes with her or the family." It sounded so mobster, but was said so sweetly.

I couldn't help but laugh. "I'm glad I'm running into all of the right people here in Alaska."

"There aren't too many wrong people here in town. How long will you be here?" The waitress dropped off waters and Mandy ordered two specials before I had a chance to look at the menu. I smiled because I trusted her. I felt safe with her, too. The women of Alaska were proving to be quite remarkable. Brynn, Cee, and Mandy. I had all but forgotten about Nita, the waitress who just spoiled my list.

"It depends. Probably around three weeks. Maybe longer. I don't want the entire story to be about Dustin Collings so I'm trying to figure out a way to integrate some local color or general fishing knowledge." If I had to focus entirely on Dustin, my old job might not be worth it. At least Erin was giving me some space to develop the story.

"I can see why. He doesn't seem like the nicest person. Adding another angle will probably keep more readers engaged."

"That's what I'm hoping. Of course, I'm pretty sure every angle about Alaska has been covered."

Mandy smiled and nodded. "Alaska does get a lot of press. Do you enjoy writing nature stories?"

I wanted to tell her the truth, but I toned down the vehemence. "This is proving to be something different than what I normally write."

"What do you normally write about?" The question I had been waiting for. Nobody wanted to hang out with a self-absorbed snob, but since she asked, I felt obligated to answer.

"Do you know *Mainstream* magazine?" I wondered what interest a librarian from Anchorage might have in celebrities.

"I think I've seen it at the grocery store in the check-out line. It's a celebrity magazine, right?"

I was happy she didn't compare us to *People Magazine* like Brynn did. "Yes. I write for them. I interview movie stars, singers, and sports celebrities. It's a lot of fun, but I've worked hard to get where I am." I felt like I had to qualify myself and my success.

"It sounds like you enjoy it. Did you volunteer to write the story or were you assigned it?" she asked. Good question. I was so excited to talk about my old job that I forgot about why I was in Alaska in the first place.

"My boss wanted something different so she sent me. I'm not a Dustin Collings fan, but I guess she thought that would be an asset to the story." Mandy didn't need to know my history. I hated that if you googled my name, the lawsuit was on the first page of the search.

"Tell me about your life here in Anchorage. Are you from here?" I asked.

"Born and raised. Several generations actually. I went to school in California, but returned after graduation. I missed my family and my home so I came back. I also had a girlfriend who missed me." There it was. The confession. I loved every word she said.

"Are you still with your girlfriend?" I was too nosy not to ask.

"I'm not with her anymore, but I'm married. Lisa is the best thing that ever happened to me. We've been married ten years." She was in love. It was all over her face. Her features softened and she got a faraway look in her eye.

"That's wonderful. I love happy endings. I'd love one. I just haven't met the right woman." Mandy didn't ask, but I felt the need to out myself to strengthen our new bond. Maybe I had met the right woman, but I was too focused on myself and my career to pay attention. An image of Nikki Toles flashed through my mind. She always showed up at the wrong time. I wasn't in love with her. She was just the only person to call it off on her terms, not mine. That irked me to no end.

When the specials were dropped on the table, I looked at Mandy in shock. I couldn't see a single inch of my plate. It was covered in breaded halibut, crinkled fries, and a few lemon wedges. I was expecting a lightly grilled halibut. I should've read the special scrawled on the blackboard on the wall.

"There's no way I can eat all of this." I didn't even want to think of all of the calories on this plate. It smelled delicious though. A few bites wouldn't hurt. "Is that real butter?" Mandy nodded.

"Real butter and real grease." She grabbed the ketchup from the table and poured a healthy portion into a tiny bowl the waitress dropped off.

"How do you stay so thin and eat like you do?" My question was probably ruder than I intended, but she took it in stride and laughed.

"I'm not that thin. I just have a healthy metabolism." She reached for two more fries. She was going to be a bad influence on me. "You'll have to come back on Friday. It's salmon day and definitely healthier. If you taste all of the fish you're supposed to write about, you'll write a better story."

"Good idea," I said. I meant it. How many different kinds of fish could there be in Alaska?

"I have a better idea. Why don't you come over to our house for dinner one night this weekend? Lisa's family has a fishing boat and I can guarantee you the freshest fish in the area. What does your Sunday look like?"

"I'm wide open. My interview with Dustin isn't for a few days. I just got here yesterday and kind of overwhelmed by what to do first and where to go," I said.

"When we get back to the library, I'll give you directions. We live in town, only a few miles from here." She pointed at my plate. "Look at you. You must have been hungry."

I looked down in mild horror. I had eaten most of the fish and half of the fries, and I wasn't even close to being done. I placed my fork down with regret. "It was delicious." I stopped myself from counting the calories. This was, as Mandy so righteously put it, all in the name of research.

Chapter Six

One of the lakes Brynn circled on one of the maps was within walking distance of the cabin. The wide, gravel path was well maintained. I felt safe. Cee recommended I carry some sort of weapon so I opted for bear spray from the general store down the street. The guy who sold it to me had a hard time not laughing. He recommended a gun. I rolled my eyes at him. I bought a walking stick, too, hoping that it would serve as a weapon if my luck with animals continued.

Cee told me to take both Murphy and King with me. How could I say no to this sweet woman who gave me the deal of a lifetime? Plus, she informed me that the dogs went to the lake all the time and I would actually be going with them, not vice versa. I agreed and off we went. Murphy bounced around and chased anything that moved. King stayed by my side until we reached the lake, then took off to play with Murphy.

I introduced myself to two men who were working on a dock in desperate need of repairs. Bob, dressed in Carhartt bibs and wading boots, looked like he just walked away from getting his mug shot taken. His unkempt, grizzly beard covered most of his face and a good portion of his neck. Gene, his older friend whose clean-shaven face was mapped with long and deep lines, joked and laughed with Bob. They were getting ready for the upcoming fishing season. I was somewhat afraid of them, but Murphy and

King trusted them. I told them what I was working on and they were both receptive to being interviewed.

Mentally, I felt high and happy that I was getting some strong background on fishing culture in Alaska. Physically, I wanted to cry. I limped over to a log that served as a bench and carefully removed my hiking boots and peeled off my thin, but cute otter socks. I didn't wear the thick boot socks because it messed with the look of my outfit. I regretted that poor decision. The back of both heels were raw with blisters, as well as the sides of both big toes. I didn't want to put the boots back on. I sat on the log for at least a half an hour feeling sorry for myself. After an hour, the dogs disappeared, and the specks off in the distance that were Bob and Gene eventually vanished. At least I had water and trail mix in my pack and I knew I would easily find my way back to the cabin. I tried not to get worked up over my misfortune again, but I couldn't help it. I'd done everything wrong in Alaska. My second full day and I couldn't even count the number of times I'd fucked up. I felt miserable. My feet were on fire and I wanted to dip them into the lake, but knowing my luck, I would slip and fall in. I tried not to think about being the only one out here or that every time I heard a noise, I thought it was a moose or bear. I wiped the tears away, pissed at my highs and lows.

"Somebody called the sanctuary and reported the sounds of a whimpering, dying animal coming from the lake. I thought I would check it out." Brynn walked down the hill and sat beside me on the makeshift bench. I tried to look like I hadn't been crying, but it was useless.

"Guilty. How did you find me?"

"Cee called. She said you left with Murphy and King, but didn't return with them so she was a little concerned. Given your history, I decided to check in to make sure you didn't have any run-ins with other animals," she said.

"I'm a complete mess. Again." I pointed at my neatly manicured feet marred by angry blisters. Brynn reached down, carefully lifted one of my legs, and placed it across her lap.

She gingerly moved my foot back and forth and looked at the blisters. "These are bad. Can you walk? They look like they might break open at any second. Do you have any medicine at the cabin or band aids?" I shook my head. "I have a first aid kit in the car if you want to…" She trailed off, knowing full well I was going nowhere. "Hang tight here for a few minutes. I'll be back."

I didn't cry again until she was out of sight. I was sure she'd never met anyone like me. I was a wimp. A true girly girl afraid of her own shadow. That wasn't a good thing. So much for making a good first impression on her. I was so disappointed in myself. For ten minutes, I pouted. Ten minutes after that I started to get worried. Did Brynn blow me off? Great. I was mangled and vulnerable to hungry animals just waking up from deep hibernation. I looked up when I heard a quiet hum of a motor and almost started crying again as Brynn made her way toward me, driving a golf cart.

"Hop in. This is the quickest way to get you back without breaking your blisters open."

"I have no idea how I would've survived the last couple days without you, Brynn." I limped over to the passenger side and crawled in. At least I didn't have blisters on the bottom of my feet. "Did Cee really call you?" Brynn reached out and playfully tapped my knee. It was a gentle touch, but my body responded delightfully. My blisters were momentarily forgotten.

"She said she was worried about you. I was in the neighborhood and thought I would do a search and rescue," she said.

"I'm so happy you did. I wasn't looking forward to the walk back to the cabin and contemplated dying right there on that log."

"You don't want to give up and die. Too many carnivores out here. Let's try to keep your body perfect and alive for at least another sixty years." She said I was perfect. Well, my body was and I would take that.

"I could never survive here. I've never been camping. I've only been to the mountains a few times in my life," I said.

"How do you stay in such good shape?" That was the second time she alluded to my body in a good way. My disposition about my life was improving with every compliment.

"I have a personal trainer."

"Your trainer needs you to pack on a few pounds. You would blow away in a windstorm around here," she said.

I frowned. So was she attracted to me or not? "I can't gain any more weight. The camera adds ten pounds and sometimes when I do video casts for our site, I look like a whale."

Brynn groaned. "You've got to be kidding me. You could easily put on thirty pounds and it would hardly show."

I turned my head to look out at the scenery. I hid my smile. Once I regained my composure, I turned to face her. The cabin was in sight. I needed to make my move and make it quick. "Did you decide on a place for dinner yet? I feel like after this save, I might owe you my firstborn."

"At this point, you might be right. I think with your blisters, you should stay off of your feet for a day or two so I can always grab dinner out and bring it back if you want." That was an even better idea.

"That sounds great. I'm honestly not sure I could go out. At least I was able to get some work done before breaking down. I met two fishermen working on a rickety dock and they let me interview them. They said the same thing you did about the lack of activity. They recommended that I head down to Homer," I said.

Brynn pulled up to the front of the cabin, as close to the two steps as she could. "It's kind of early for salmon fishing, but the commercial fishermen are out year round and a lot of them do private excursions. I could give you a few names and maybe they would be willing to talk to you. Free press is free press." She rushed to my side and held her hand out to help me out of the cart. Her grip was strong, yet her hands soft. My mind was flooded with visions of us having sex and how strong and careful she would be with me. I shivered. "Are you cold?" The flushed look that was on my face was probably enough to let her know I wasn't. She cleared her throat and let my hand drop. I grabbed the bannister like it was planned all along, but I immediately missed her warmth.

"Once I get inside and take a hot shower, I'll be good."

"There should be a first aid kit in the bathroom with band aids and cream that will help with your blisters." She slowly backed down the stairs as if she wanted to run away quickly.

"You don't have to go. I mean, if you need to get back to work, I understand, but you are more than welcome to come inside and visit for a bit." I tried to make the offer sincere by offering her my reserved-for-special-occasions smile, but it didn't have the effect on her that I wanted it to. I was lonely and I needed company. Besides, she was beautiful and spending some quality time with her that didn't involve her rescuing animals or me would've been nice. I tried hard not to pout when she continued walking to the golf cart.

"I need to finish my shift at the sanctuary. Plus I need to get the cart back to Cee." I nodded and hated that I felt tears spring up. Brynn must have seen it too because she softened immediately. "Hey, I tell you what. You take care of you and I'll come back with dinner in an hour or so."

That brightened my mood immediately. "I could use the company," I said.

She nodded. "Can I bring a friend?"

I tried not to look surprised, but I couldn't help it. "Um, sure, I guess." Great. My night was turning into shit. Like I wanted to sit around and watch Brynn and her guest hit it off when in reality I wanted to hit it off with her. Just me.

"Okay, give me a couple hours and I'll be back." Her smile. Damn. It was higher on the left side, almost a smirk, and sexy as hell. I forgave her solely based on her smile. I waved when she drove off, then hobbled back inside.

I called Dustin Collings to confirm our appointment in two days, but I got his voice mail again. I left another message explaining who I was and that I was excited to meet him and tell the world about his new show. I rolled my eyes the entire time, but I sounded sincere. If he didn't call me back soon, I was going to be annoyed.

Half an hour later, Erin called. I was on the couch, almost asleep, my laptop across my chest. "Hey, boss. What's going on?"

"I have an update about your interview."

"Good. Did he contact the office? I just left him another message."

"His agent called. It isn't great news."

I sat up and set my laptop on the side table. "What's going on?"

"Dustin cancelled. He's somewhere in the Pacific either shooting an episode or reshooting scenes for his show. The agent was pretty vague."

"Are you fucking kidding me?" I was livid. Everything I did and suffered through was for naught. "What a jerk."

"Yeah, so that story is dead." She didn't sound too upset. The hairs on the back of my neck stood up. Again.

"Do you want me to come back?" I already knew the answer.

"No. You're already up there so you should stay."

"Why?" That sounded rude. I started over. "Are you setting up another interview?"

"No, but between the Alaska advertisements and the money we have already spent on this story, Travis and *A&A* can't afford another journalist and another story. I think you can still come up with something good. Maybe incorporate more wildlife in your story."

Sure, ask for the impossible, I thought. We hung up and I tossed my phone on the couch in frustration. My shoulders slumped. I was stuck here without a definite story. At least Dustin would have been easy.

I gingerly stood up and stretched. I ached everywhere. A shower was the only thing that was going to make me feel good. I popped a few ibuprofen to manage the throbbing of my feet. I officially hated everything about this day.

CHAPTER SEVEN

Oh, my God, Brynn. What's that?" She carried a brown bag of what I presumed was our dinner, but also had a fuzzy animal perched on her shoulder. It was a small raccoon, but it was so unbelievable that I couldn't wrap my head around it.

"This is my guest. Meet Wally, a six-month-old raccoon who hates to be alone. He's well-behaved and I promise he won't be a problem," she said. I should've been excited that her guest wasn't another woman, but animals unnerved me and I wasn't too excited about a wild one in my cabin. "He's more like a dog, or a cat." I stood completely out of the way of both of them when Brynn walked in.

"Tell me he didn't touch our dinner," I said.

"I promise. He was in the seat next to me. Dinner was in the back. No live animal parts touched these dead animal parts." Her tasteless joke made me smile.

"I'm sorry. I'm just not used to animals or pets. He's pretty cute though," I said.

Wally clutched Brynn tightly, but his eyes darted wildly around the cabin. It was just a matter of time before he got comfortable here. Brynn handed me a treat to give to Wally. I was hesitant because as cute and small as he was, his claws and teeth looked pretty big to me.

"It's okay. He's gentler than an old dog. I want you to get comfortable with him and see that he's not a threat at all. He's even friendly with Cee's dogs and they normally want to kill raccoons. I think they know he's safe. You did mention earlier that you thought King and Murphy were excellent judges of character."

I carefully offered the treat to Wally, and cringed as I waited for him to scratch me to get to it. Ever so gently, as if in slow motion, he stretched his paws out and tapped my hand before lightly taking the treat. I was amazed.

"Why's he tapping me?" I could have asked the question a better way, one that didn't make both of us embarrassed, but Brynn was nice enough to answer and ignored the innuendo.

"I think it's his way of saying he isn't going to hurt you. He's remarkable," Brynn said. She placed him gently on the wood floor and although he was curious, he stayed close to her legs. "How are your blisters?"

"Much better. I have them bandaged up. I'm not going to even put on my boots until I absolutely have to and hopefully not until tomorrow."

"I'm glad. They looked painful."

I nodded. "So what's in the bag?"

Brynn raised her eyebrow at me and headed over to the kitchen. "Only the best burgers in Alaska. I got three different kinds. Beef, wild salmon, and halibut. I wasn't sure if you actually ate meat, so I took a gamble."

"I don't eat a lot of it, but I do eat it. And I decided yesterday I needed to eat more of the food here so I'm in." I watched as she organized dinner on plates, splitting all three burgers and homemade chips. Wally was close by, lifting his tiny masked face toward the food, his nose darting back and forth between Brynn and the counter. It smelled delicious. My stomach rumbled. "Thank you for getting dinner. I would've eaten a protein bar just to avoid putting on my shoes to drive somewhere." I accepted the plate she handed me and headed over to the table. "Would you like some wine or beer or a soda? I have a few things in the refrigerator." She grabbed us both beers and joined me. Wally was quiet, but right at her feet. "Will he eat this for dinner, too?"

"I have food for him out in the car. He'll get his dinner after we're done. He's pretty happy so he doesn't beg a lot. Of course, he's only been to a few different houses so I don't know how he's going to behave during our meal."

We settled into dinner and an easy conversation about her job and what I'd been working on the last two days. She was incredibly charming and sexy in her jeans, flannel shirt, and hiking boots. Relaxed and at ease. I decided to press more about her personal life because the only thing I knew about her was that she had a pet raccoon and moved here when she was relatively young.

"How old were you when you came here? I was talking to Mandy at the library yesterday and she said a lot of people in Alaska are from somewhere else." I hoped my question came across as an innocent conversation question and not an inquisition. I wanted to know more about her.

"I like Mandy. She's nice." Brynn sat back and continued eating. She didn't offer any more information so I pressed on.

"Yeah, we had lunch yesterday. She invited me over Sunday night for dinner," I said. I tried to gauge Brynn's reaction and was met with a wall. Brynn Coleman was great at masking her feelings.

"I came to Alaska about twelve years ago. I caught my girlfriend with somebody else and it snowballed out of control. I was just done with that life. I got in my car and kept driving until the road ended." She shrugged as if it was as easy for her as a trip to the mall, but it had to have devastated her.

"Ouch. That's rough. At least you picked a beautiful spot to end up. Cold and full of crazy animals, but very pretty." I tried to lighten the mood. It worked. There was that crooked and adorable smile. I hovered on the border of excitement and confusion at the way she looked at me. It made my palms sweat and my heart accelerate. I couldn't decide if she was interested in me or saw me as a charity case.

"Well, if we're confessing, I have a doozy of a story about a sort of ex-girlfriend and why I'm here in Alaska." I took a long swallow of beer and told her the story of Nikki Toles, leaving nothing out. The bare bones of my debacle was on the internet anyway. It wasn't as if she couldn't have found out for herself and filled in the obvious blanks. I slept with a married woman and got sued for it.

Brynn clinked her longneck against mine. "Let's find you the best story ever here so that you can get back to the life you miss." She was sincere, but it rubbed me the wrong way a little. I didn't want Brynn to think I was shallow. I wasn't, but I also recognized that I wasn't the idealist that I had been fresh out of college. My career had pushed me out of the realm of a reality where the rest of the world lived. My so-called friends were famous and had their own agendas. I didn't know my neighbors or the name of the guy who did my dry cleaning every week. Every single week I dropped off my suits and shirts and I thought I was friendly enough, but I seriously wracked my brain trying to come up with his name. Nothing.

"I'm not too worried. I'm here for three weeks and I'm bound to come up with something," I said. Thankfully, I'd already started researching. There was so much information, I was sure I could write something in a few short days, but I promised Erin I would help her help Travis so I was taking my time. If nothing else, I valued my word.

Brynn finished her half of the salmon burger in four bites. She was slender and all muscle and I wondered where her calories went. After watching her rescue the owl the other day, I figured she needed a ton of energy to do her job.

She looked up from her plate; her gray eyes sparkled and held my gaze for several moments before smiling. "I love food," she said. There was a tiny bit of ketchup perched on the corner of her mouth that she quickly wiped away.

"I can see that. I was just thinking that you probably need a lot of protein and carbs to save animals. You crawled all over the place to get to that owl. You probably used more energy in just one rescue than I use all day sitting at my desk." My appetite was no match for hers.

"It's hard not to be physical in Alaska. My best workout is chopping wood. It's cardio, builds upper body strength, and increases stamina. I wish I knew about chopping wood when I was a swimmer at Florida State. I would've won every heat for sure." My mouth dropped open. I used her explanation to openly study her body. Broad shoulders, tiny waist, fantastic height. Perfect build for a swimmer.

"Florida State, huh? Great swimmers there." I didn't want to push her even though I was dying to know the full story. She left Florida and drove straight to Alaska? Did she walk away from everything? I couldn't help myself. I need to know more. "So, are you hiding out?" She looked confused. I shook my head. "Does your family know you're here? Is that too rude? I'm sorry." For a split second, Brynn looked dejected, but she covered it quickly.

"Well, I kind of left because of my family so I never made it a point to tell them. I'm sure if they wanted to find me, they could." Dinner just got a thousand times more interesting. The reporter in me was fighting to ask a million questions, but I didn't want to make Brynn uncomfortable. She was going to tell me her story, but on her terms. I could wait.

"I'm not on great terms with my family either. My parents weren't overly excited when I moved to California, but I knew what I wanted to do with my life. They wanted me to settle down and get married right after college, but my Midwestern upbringing made me want to leave as soon as possible."

Brynn chuckled wryly. "My dysfunctional family made me want to leave as soon as possible. I actually left in the middle of the night in the middle of a semester."

I drank my beer to shut my mouth. I nodded coolly and finished the beef burger. "That was brave. You must have been what? Eighteen? Nineteen?"

"Nineteen. Sophomore year, but my problems started when I was a freshman." She was momentarily distracted by Wally who was getting impatient for his dinner. "I need to feed this guy. I'm going to run out to the Jeep and get his food." She headed for the door.

I panicked. "Wait. You're going to leave me alone with him?" "Yes, for about ten seconds." She winked. "Or maybe thirty minutes." She closed the door behind her. Wally and I looked at one another. He seemed as wary of me as I was of him. He waddled over to me and put his paws on my leg. A part of me wanted to reach down and pet him because I wanted to know what he felt like, and another part wanted me to shake him off my leg and run like hell. He was kind of cute with his soulful eyes and a fuzzy mask. The longer we kept eye contact, the more comfortable I was with him.

"Wally, are you hungry?" I asked. I swore he knew exactly what I said because he got animated and reached up at my plate, then pulled back, then reached up again. I handed him a chip. He delicately took it and heartily chomped. "You eat like your mama."

"Are you talking about me?" Brynn asked. I was just about to pet him when she returned with Wally's food and ruined my moment. The minute he saw her, he whimpered and scurried up her leg. "See? He hates being alone. This is why I have no social life." I didn't know if that was her way of telling me she was single, or her just sharing information between new friends.

"I'm glad you brought him by. It's a little weird for me, but in a good way. A week ago, I couldn't imagine having dinner with a pet raccoon. Not only did I just feed him a chip, but now I want to touch him." I watched as Brynn placed Wally on her shoulder and how careful he was with her hair as he held on to her.

She reached up and scooped him into her arms so he was cradled against her body. "Come here. He has the softest belly." I headed her way not just because I wanted to touch him, but I wanted to be close to her and this was an excuse to be in her personal space. "Here. Give me your hand." She held my hand and pulled it down with hers until we were both touching his furry belly. The warmth from her touch elevated my heart rate and I wondered if she could hear it pounding as we stood close. "See? He's a sweetheart. He likes the attention." Wally leaned forward to smell my hands. I sighed when Brynn's fingers left mine and I was the only one rubbing his fur. "Your eyes have copper flecks in them. Almost the same color as your hair."

Brynn's nearness was both unnerving and desirable. We were a foot apart. If it wasn't for Wally's paws reaching between our faces, I'm sure she would've kissed me right then. Or I would've kissed her. Her lips were full and I wanted to taste her softness.

"Looks like Wally wants dinner," I said. I took a step back and I swore I heard her sigh.

"Can I borrow a bowl?" Her voice was shaky, but her gaze was strong. Her gray eyes were dark, almost black as she stared at me. There were unspoken words between us. I bit my lip, letting her know I was thinking about the kiss that never happened, and she visibly swallowed. It seemed we were both turned on just by standing close.

"Um. Yes. Let me just grab you one." I walked into the kitchenette area. The cabin was suddenly very small and I was aware of her every move. She followed me over to the counter and took the bowl from my hands. Wally was an animated hot mess when he realized it was dinnertime. He scurried from one of Brynn's shoulders to the other.

"Settle down, buddy." Brynn peeled him off of her shirt and placed him at her feet. He clutched her boots and looked at her. It was sweet and I melted a little bit. I was starting to fall for the little guy even though he prevented what I thought would be a mind-blowing kiss. Brynn's lips were the kind of lips that would blossom with a kiss. Soft, yet demanding. I stifled a shiver. She noticed. "Are you chilled? Do you want me to start a fire?"

"I'm okay. Thank you though." I was worried that a fire might scare Wally. Funny how just thirty minutes before, I was scared of him. Now, I was raccoon-proofing my entire cabin. We watched him eat and I smiled at his real appreciation for food. "So what exactly is he eating? Because it doesn't smell the greatest."

"I don't want him to get too far removed from food he could forage for in the wild, so some berries, fish, eggs, nuts, and some grain-free kibble as filler." Brynn motioned me away from Wally.

We grabbed our plates and sat on the sofa facing one another. "He'll find us when he's done."

"I'm surprised at him. He's so good and interactive. I guess I didn't expect that at all. Actually, I never gave raccoons a second thought until tonight. What'll happen to him?" I was afraid of the answer. I wanted only good things for Wally.

"Well, most likely, he will live his life out at the sanctuary and with me. He will be a greeter for us once he gets used to crowds. People like wild animals, especially ones they can feel safe around. It's still important to teach people that even though he's super cute, most raccoons are wild and not as nice as Wally."

We finished our food and Brynn put our dishes in the sink. When she returned to the sofa, she pulled the pillow out from behind her and placed it on her lap. I leaned back. Our fur ball barrier from before had been replaced with a sage and maroon patterned cushion. My night was not looking up.

"Does the sanctuary do well, financially I mean? Do you get a lot of outside support?" I was curious about the costs associated with running a refuge. Feeding and caring for wild animals had to be expensive. There was so much I didn't know about wildlife sanctuaries.

"We're government funded from the unlikeliest of places. Clean energy promotion, restoration projects here in Alaska. We have some wealthy supporters who donate every year." Brynn looked down and started playing with the seams on the pillow. "If you don't have any plans for tomorrow, I can take you around the sanctuary if you're really interested." She was obviously nervous.

I smiled and wondered when the last time she had a date was. Not that this was a date, but I wondered about the last time she opened herself up to someone.

Wally climbed on the sofa and looked back and forth between us. "Are you all done?" I asked. I was comfortable with him, but we weren't on cuddle terms just yet. I pointed to Brynn and smiled when he went over to her. She moved the pillow and Wally crawled on her lap to play. "He's an amazing little guy."

The smile on Brynn's face couldn't have been any bigger. "I'm so proud of him, but I can't take any credit. He's just wonderful," she said.

We talked for two more hours until Brynn stifled a few yawns. I reluctantly kicked them out, but not before agreeing to meet Brynn at the sanctuary in the morning. I wasn't in the mood to drive four or five hours to Homer for halibut fishing, and I was interested in visiting the sanctuary after spending so much time talking about it tonight.

"Thanks for the hospitality. We both appreciated it." Brynn scooped up Wally and leaned toward me. My heart leapt in my chest and I inhaled sharply at the thought of her kissing me, but she turned at the last second so that I was face to face with Wally and had to pet him instead. As cute as the gesture was, and as charming as Wally was, I just wanted her lips on mine.

CHAPTER EIGHT

Every road looked the same in Alaska. I panicked even though I could still see some of Cee's cabins through the trees. Visions of moose danced in my head and I automatically slowed the SUV. There wasn't a line of cars behind me so I didn't care. The speed limit was only a suggestion. My trip was about ten minutes away so I relaxed and turned on the music. By the time I found the University of Anchorage's alternative station, I was at the sanctuary. I took a couple of deep breaths after I parked. I was too excited to see Brynn and I didn't want her to know. I thought about Wally and grinned. I grabbed the camera and climbed out of my new ride. It was amazing how much safer I felt sitting so high. I was seriously rethinking my tiny convertible back home.

Brynn pushed through the door and headed straight for me. "Hi. Right on time."

I looked her up and down and smiled. Her uniform was doing a number on my libido. I didn't hide my appreciation. She didn't seem to mind my appraisal. Where was this cocky woman last night when it was time to say good-bye?

"Where's Wally?" I shaded my eyes from the sun so I could see her. She theatrically put her hand on her heart and took a step back.

"And here I thought you were here to see me." The twinkle in her eye was adorable. The smirk she was trying to cover up? Melted me. It also added to my confusion.

"You're the bonus." Fuck it. I decided to flirt back and see if that changed anything. I got a confident wink. I almost threw my hands in the air. In front of the world, she was self-assured. In the privacy of my cabin, she was reserved and respectful. I didn't need either of those. I needed her strong hands on my body and her full lips marking my neck. I wanted something to happen with her. A kiss, a fling, a simple touch. Something that would get her out of my system and make me stop thinking about her.

"Well, let's grab a truck and head out." Brynn directed me to a pickup truck.

"Are we not going to walk around?"

"Only if you want to get mauled by a bear." She shrugged her shoulders like it was no big deal.

"That would be a no." I climbed in, thankful that even though my blisters were heavily bandaged, I wasn't going to have to walk everywhere today.

"Put your seat belt on," Brynn said.

"Really? Are we going to run into traffic out in the vastness of a sanctuary?" I looked around and saw nothing but open fields, mountains, and only a few hints of civilization.

"Maybe a moose."

My seat belt was secured in three seconds flat. Brynn's shoulders shook with quiet laughter. I shot her a stern look that did nothing to suppress her teasing. She nodded slowly like she just burned me with the best joke ever. I rolled my eyes and looked out of the window so she wouldn't see my smile.

"Is Wally not going to be joining us?"

"I have my hands full with you. I don't want to have to worry about him, too." Brynn waved to one of the rangers who opened both sets of gates for us.

We headed off into the unknown. Well, at least to me. I was excited to see the different animals and hear their stories. Last night, Brynn told me about some of them, but I wanted to know everything.

"I packed us a lunch. We're probably going to be out here a few hours if you have the time."

"I have nothing planned but you today," I said.

Brynn shot me the sexiest look. I felt my body swell in all the right places. She was clearly interested in me, but wouldn't do anything about it. I hated making the first move, but I hated my body swollen with no relief in sight even more. I hadn't been with a woman since Nikki and I was ready to explode. One night with Brynn would be fantastic. Just what I needed, but that wasn't a possibility. She was entirely too nice and sweet for a quick lay.

"What's your favorite thing? What makes this your ideal job?" I eased into the interview. Brynn was relaxed and calm and I wanted this vibe to continue. While she talked, I snapped photos during the drive. I had no idea where we were headed, but I trusted her. She had done nothing but save my ass since I got here.

"The best part about my job is that I'm not chained to a desk. I work with nature. I love going to work every day. I love when we can save an animal and release it back into the wilderness. Sometimes they have to live out the rest of their lives here and while it's a pretty good replica of life, it's not the same as absolute freedom," she says. She scowled and I knew she was thinking of when animals couldn't be saved.

I redirected the conversation. "Tell me about Owlie. What happened to him?"

"Owlie? That's what you named him?" She looked at me and her smile returned. "He's going to be okay. We'll release him close to Mrs. Wilson's place. His wing's sprained. Another few days and he'll get back out there." I reached over and touched her forearm. She jerked, but kept her arm on the steering wheel.

"That was great what you did. I was happy to be a part of it. An observer, but still I saw it. You are very good and patient at what you do." I didn't move my hand for a few seconds. I felt her relax under my touch.

"I couldn't have planned it better if I tried. Owlie was an easy one. Most of the time I'm wrestling with different animals trying to get them into the Jeep or get them sedated so we can help them," she said.

"How did you get Melissa and Yogi? Do you get a lot of bears?"

"We got them when they were cubs. Poachers killed their mother. My guess is the poachers tried to get them, too, but they were smaller targets and got away. Yogi was shot in the shoulder so now he walks with a limp," Brynn said.

"Is poaching a problem?" I asked. Geographically, Alaska was so vast and the population seemed so small.

"It's a horrible problem. There are so many guidelines and restrictions on hunting and so many hunters just don't care. To them, it's about making money selling pelts, antlers, and anything they can make a buck on. It's like suddenly we're back in the eighteen hundreds and it's a free for all." Brynn's knuckles tightened against the steering wheel. I gave her time before I broached the subject again. She continued without any encouragement from me. "We know most of the hunters around here. There are people who come here just to hunt and their guides are sticklers for the rules, but every once in a while, a new hunting business will open and we constantly check in with them to ensure they are hunting by the rules and it's not a front for something illegal." she says.

"What are bear cubs like?"

"They are actually bigger than you think. Remember Tuffy and how large he was? Well, cubs are big animals who think they are small. Yogi and Melissa were both defensive. I mean, could you blame them? Humans killed their mother and I'm sure our scent was all around the scene. It took a long time for them to warm up to us. Even now I stay in the truck when they are close. These animals are still wild, even though they are kind of stuck here." Brynn pulled over to an area where I saw three bears foraging.

"You have more than just Melissa and Yogi?" I leaned out the window and took a ton of photos. They were beautiful. "Can I step out of the truck to get a better picture?"

"Absolutely not. You have to stay inside, but I can get closer if you want," she said. I nodded and sat back down. I felt like a kid at a zoo, only this zoo was the size of a city. "Tell me about the other bears in here. I know about the twins. What about these guys?" "These are some older bears we've had since before I started. Two were injured, and one was actually born here. They haven't been out of hibernation long and are trying to put on weight by eating everything they can." We sat and watched the bears dig around for food. It was amazing to see nature this close and personal. I switched out my lens for the telephoto so I could capture facial expressions and see them eat. One of the grizzlies was eating a stalk with budding blue flowers on the stem.

"What is that one eating?"

"The Alaskan state flower is the forget-me-not. Bears like eating their roots." Brynn was the ideal person to show nature to me with her experience and knowledge. She was respectful and didn't take it for granted.

"Brynn, thank you so much. This is incredible." I was happy being quiet and just being in nature like I'd never experienced it before, raw and unblemished. Yes, it kicked my ass, but Brynn made it so accessible for me.

Even though we didn't see a lot of animals the deeper we drove into the sanctuary, the view was gorgeous. There was a photo op at every angle. Everywhere I looked was a scene one would find in a painting. There were so many different types of trees, wild prairie grasses, and boulders that popped up in the foreground before introducing the massive ranges in the distance. Brynn named the different mountains and I took notes. It would be beautiful here in summer because it was spectacular in the middle of spring.

"Look. Your favorite." She pointed past me to a few moose loitering through thin, budding bushes. I cringed. She laughed. "Want to eat lunch? It's not much, but it should hold us over until tonight." She put the truck in park and motioned for me to step out.

I felt free the moment my boots hit the ground. Brynn opened two folding chairs in the back of her truck and held out her hand to help me up. "You can see more up here."

"I would eat lunch here every day." I slowly turned in my spot to soak it all in. There was something magical about the sanctuary. It had all the beauty of Alaska, but was uniquely compelling because of the caring people and wounded animals. I wondered if I could work it into my *A&A* story.

Brynn nudged me to get my attention and handed me a brown bag and a bottle of water. "I do eat here most days. Not here in this spot, but I usually take my lunch on the go," she said.

"Do you ever get lonely?" I asked the question before I thought about it. "I mean, is there a partner you have here at the sanctuary?" I hoped that was innocent enough. Yes, I wanted to know if she buddied up with another woman for fun stuff, but I was asking about work. I don't know that I could go so long without human interaction.

"I'm never alone." She nodded her head to something behind me. I turned and stared at a small herd of eight animals lumbering our way.

"Are those buffalo?" I was stunned.

"They are wood bison. We have a few calves that were born recently. Here. You might want to take some pics." Brynn handed me my camera. I couldn't think about anything other than gaping at them. They didn't care that we were there. They walked within about twenty feet of the truck. I took a step back until I was almost leaning on Brynn. She stood behind me, her body tall, strong, and close. I felt her warm breath on my ear and tried hard not to tremble at her nearness. "Don't worry about them. Just be quiet and they'll be on their merry way."

I held my breath as one of the calves curiously veered in our direction and was swiftly corralled back to the herd by his mother. He snorted and she was quick to respond with a loud stomp of her hoof and noise that reminded me of the sounds Martha made at Tuffy. I turned to Brynn, excited and invigorated, after they lumbered past. "Did you see how that baby wanted to come over to us? He was so curious."

I was too excited to pay attention to her when she tucked a piece of hair behind my ear, and I hardly noticed how close she was to me as I told her all about it. When her thumb rubbed the soft skin just below my bottom lip, everything stopped. I realized we were only inches apart and my stomach dropped while my heart jumped. When her other hand reached up to rest against my cheek, I leaned into her touch and stopped talking. Her eyes were dark like they were the night before, her lips slightly apart. Her breath was warm on my mouth and I silently begged her to kiss me.

When I finally felt the softness of her full lips press against mine, I whimpered with the need for more. I closed the gap between us so our bodies were close and swayed against her when she deepened the kiss. She tasted warm, and soft, and I moaned when our tongues finally touched. We teased one another, both of us taking control and giving it at the same time.

Her hands slid down my back and rested on my hips. I felt myself moving against her, unabashedly, wanting the friction of this beautiful woman against me. I wasn't used to waiting so I took the opportunity to throw my entire self into our kiss. I slipped my hands under her jacket, marveling at her warmth even though there was still a layer of clothing between my touch and her skin.

She ran a hand up my back until her fingertips pressed into my neck gently, yet possessively. She was confident and smooth. Gone was the awkward woman who was uncomfortable around me. This kiss lasted seconds, minutes, hours. I had no idea. I lost track of time in her arms. I didn't care about the mountains, the animals, or where I was. I only cared about Brynn and this kiss I had wanted since the moment I saw her. I frowned when she pulled away. I opened my eyes to her sexy smile and a new playful twinkle in her eye.

"Well, that was nice," she said. Her tongue darted out to lick her lips. I did the same and still tasted her on my mouth.

"Nice and unexpected." I felt awkward when she let me go, so I adjusted my camera until my body settled down and my clit wasn't throbbing. Brynn knew how to kiss. She had full, soft lips for a reason.

"Are you ready for more?" she asked.

I hoped she meant kissing me senseless, but she meant continuing with the tour. I prayed my disappointment didn't show. We climbed back in the truck and headed toward the mountains. We were both quiet. I was quiet because I couldn't decide if I should jump her now, or at least wait until we had fewer clothes on. She was probably quiet because she was regretting the kiss. I wanted to know all the reasons why she kissed me. Maybe she was overcome by the situation, too.

"Do you spend most of your time here checking on things, or out there beyond the fences?" I asked just to alleviate the silence.

"It depends on how many calls we get during the day. There are twelve full-time rangers here and several volunteers. We rotate the schedule often to try to keep everyone happy." She hadn't made eye contact with me since we got into the truck.

"Are you the only female ranger?"

"There are three women. Me, Jody, and Linda. Linda's retired and now volunteers as a tour guide at the sanctuary. We're a good family," she said.

"You drive around alone a lot. Is that normal?"

"Sometimes if the call's something greater than saving a small animal like Owlie, we pair up. It's always great when we can help, but sometimes we can't." Her voice got low and quiet. She must have carried a lot of grief doing this job.

The radio clicked on. They needed her to head to the south entrance to one of the parks because of an animal in distress. She turned to me for the first time since our kiss.

"I have to get back to the office and grab a few things. I hope you don't mind, but we have to cut this short." She looked dejected.

I just wanted to reach out and touch her to let her know that everything was going to be okay, but I couldn't make that kind of promise to her. "I understand. We can try again another time. I'll be here a while." I placed my hand on her forearm and squeezed. She flashed me a smile, but it was brief and didn't meet her eyes. This was serious. She drove fast, but carefully, and we were back to the parking lot within a few minutes.

"I'll call you soon. Stick around. Wally's probably inside and would like to see you, or you can do the touristy thing and walk around here." She dropped me off at my SUV and took off. Just like that, I was alone again. It took hours for me to get over my melancholy mood.

CHAPTER NINE

I'd wanted to call Brynn, but she never left me her business card. I could have asked Cee for her number, but I figured Brynn's afternoon went to shit and she probably needed space.

I couldn't sleep. I kept tossing and turning thinking about our kiss. Why was I so drawn to Brynn? Yes, she was definitely my type, and usually by now, people who kissed me like that were already in my bed. She confused me like no woman had before. Why was she so hesitant? Was she not into me? Wait. Did she have a girlfriend already? Did I just cause some horrific break up? No. Brynn didn't strike me as the cheating kind.

The next morning, since I was completely alone and bored, I decided to brave the drive to Homer and try my luck at gathering information for my story. The more I thought about the sanctuary, the more I thought it would make a good story, but I was afraid my attraction to Brynn was clouding my judgment. Maybe Homer's fishing community would give me some perspective. I got up early, packed an overnight bag in case I decided to stay in Homer, and took off. Slowly, of course, because my eyes darted every direction waiting for wildlife to jump out. After about thirty minutes hunched over my steering wheel in silence, I relaxed a little and leaned back in the seat. The signs every ten to twenty miles listed Homer so I doubted I'd get lost.

When I pulled into town, I already knew I was going to stay the night. Charming didn't do it justice. I parked and headed straight for the spit, a strip of land that had a line of quaint shops and fishing shacks along the water. Several men were fishing from the beach. I finally saw why people came all the way to Alaska for this sport. After talking to several shop owners who directed me to the most popular fishing tour, I signed up for a half-day trip the next morning that promised halibut galore. Six a.m. didn't sound great, but it was already too late in the day to do anything but chat with locals and fishermen on the beach. It was chilly right on the water, but the view was breathtaking and I didn't want to leave. Homer was nested within the Kenai mountain range. Eagles scavenged on the beach, a sight I had never seen. Dozens of eagles were pecking at clams, fish, and anything that floated in from the Kachemak Bay. I felt small and unimportant.

I missed lunch completely, but had dinner early and scored a room at one of the Best Westerns in town. It was clean, rustic, and I almost clapped when I saw the Wi-Fi sign in the window. I needed to plug in and find out how California was surviving without me.

Erin answered the phone herself. "Please don't tell me you're calling because you wrecked another car."

"Where's Gabrielle?" I sat down and carefully pulled off my boots. My blisters still looked ugly, but they were healing.

"Why? So you can give her the bad news. Oh, no. Now you get to deal with me."

"Hey, everything's fine. I was just checking in. And I want to know everything that's going on and everything I missed. You know, healthy gossip. I haven't been online in twenty-four hours so I'm starting to feel a little bit removed," I said.

"How's Alaska? As rural as I have it pictured in my head?" Her voice held a note of cheekiness.

I got a little defensive. "It's like no other place I've ever been. It's rural, but charming. There are animals everywhere. I could have touched an eagle on the beach just now. For the record, they are bigger in real life than you think. It's also a lot colder than I thought, but overall, I like it." Well, I liked Alaska when I was with Brynn and she was showing me her life. Branching out on my own was boring. I learned that this kind of beauty was meant to be shared. Not even the photos I took did it justice. "I sent a few photos to Lynn to add to the company intranet. Just some fun stuff that I think she would like."

"How's the story?" That was her way of asking me if I was staying on task and not taking a vacation on company time.

"I'm still leaning toward a fishing story. So much of my research was about deep-sea fishing, it seems useless to waste that information. I chartered a boat tomorrow for some halibut fishing. I figured it would be fun to cover different options for our readers. There were also guys fishing right off the beach. So much happens here. The big thing is salmon fishing. There are several different kinds and..." I trailed off because I was rambling and she was bored. I'd worked for her long enough to know silence wasn't her being polite.

"Hey, maybe you'll run into Dustin out there on the seas."

"Ha. I'd sink his boat." I had no desire to talk to the guy.

"Have you figured out an angle yet? Since you have the feature, make sure you send about ten kick-ass photos, too."

"Oh, trust me, you'll have a hard time narrowing it down to just ten," I said with confidence. Earlier, I took the money shot when one of the fishermen on the beach yanked in a giant halibut. The giant, flat fish was in the air, two feet from his outstretched arms, with the Alaskan snowcapped mountains and glaciers in the background. I almost cried when I saw the photo. If my story sucked, that photo alone would redeem me. "I feel really good about this, Erin. I'm actually excited even though every day I've been a hot mess here. This has been quite the adventure. I'm not thanking you for this assignment so don't get excited just yet." I heard her snort over the phone.

"You still have a few weeks. Keep me posted on your progress," she said.

"Let me run something by you. So, the magazine focuses on nature in general. How about I do a story on the sanctuary I've been talking about? They do such great work and I'm sure I can get tons of photos there. Plus, I can interview the director, a few of the rangers, one of the veterinarians, and locals about the importance of the place." I clutched the phone tightly as I waited for her answer. The more I'd thought about it during my drive, the more I loved the idea. I wanted Erin to know I wasn't wasting time. "I mean, I can still do a side article on fishing. I already have great photos and a lot of information. I just don't think it would be as exciting as the sanctuary." I finally shut up long enough for Erin to process my idea.

"You know what, Kennedy? That's not a bad idea. If you make the sanctuary the feature and write a fun, quirky fishing side story, I think that will work. I'll run it by Travis and text you later."

I heard the excitement in her voice and mentally high-fived myself. Screw Dustin Collings. We didn't need him. Nobody cared about him. The only people I ran into who were excited about him were tourists.

I ended the call and gathered my notes and interviews. Once I downloaded my photos, I stopped jotting things down and looked through all nine hundred and fifty-four photos. There was no way I was going to be able to narrow what I had down to just ten photos. I still had the fishing boat tomorrow which was sure to produce at least three good shots. At least I could use those for the fishing story. I already had a ton of great photos from the sanctuary.

I stopped the slideshow when I found a picture of Brynn loading food into a trough for an elk who was being treated for a hurt leg. He was confined for his own protection. Before our tour the day before, Brynn had stopped to feed the bull since the other rangers were out on calls. We weren't there for more than ten minutes, but I took at least fifty photos. The one I sent was brilliant. It was the back of Brynn with the majestic elk only a few feet away. There was so much trust going on in the photo. He trusted her not to hurt him, and she trusted him not to hurt her. Brynn was beautiful. Her shoulder muscles strained from lifting the heavy food and pouring it into the bin. The next photo was of her reaching out to the elk and him hesitantly walking into her touch. She was fearless.

I found a few more photos with her, but only one of her face. I zoomed in so I could stare at her. I couldn't tell if she was eighteen or thirty-five. She didn't have a single freckle or mole on her face. There was a tiny scar under her lip I hadn't noticed before. I wondered if it was a childhood injury, or one that happened during her swimming career. The look in her eyes still held an element of innocence.

I hated myself for googling her, but that didn't stop me from trying. I came up empty searching for Brynn Coleman so I reversed my search method. I knew she was a swimmer at Florida State twelve or thirteen years before. Finally, I found her under the name Brynn Whitfield. Why was she using the name Coleman?

I spent the next hour investigating Brynn Whitfield. In high school, she won state her junior and senior years in the butterfly and the backstroke. I found a picture of her without her swimming cap on. Her long black hair was halfway down her back. I was surprised at how feminine she looked. She was homecoming queen at Franklin High, and Student Body President. She was definitely the sweet girl next door with nothing but opportunity ahead of her. The question was what the hell happened that would make her leave everything? Catching your girlfriend with someone else was horrible, but was it bad enough to change your entire life? I couldn't imagine. Maybe that's because I never let my heart lead. Maybe I did at eighteen, but life gave me different wants and dreams as an adult. I was even more determined to find out about Brynn's past and all of her secrets.

Things I learned about myself in Alaska: I was in over my head the minute I landed on the ground, and I was just as worthless at sea. The captain gave me a bucket and sat me near the front of the boat away from the others. I was fine until we hit open waters. Open choppy waters. I clung to the side of the boat for dear life. I couldn't look anywhere but at my boots.

"I have Dramamine if you need some," the captain said to me. He looked a little crusty, but I felt like that was part of the charm. I didn't hesitate to take him up on his offer. My stomach needed to settle so that I could get to work. There were so many interesting characters on this boat and I wanted to talk to them. I gratefully accepted a bottle of water, two saltine crackers, and a Dramamine. It took over an hour to get into my system and work its magic. I also thought the clean, crisp air added to my recovery. My lungs weren't used to such purity. I was able to look up and around, but walking was still out of the question. I took remarkable photos by only moving my head. I saw all of the fish the customers caught and by the end of the trip, I wobbled over to interview them. My favorite people to talk to were Marge and Bob Cooper from Ohio.

"Even though we're retired, we felt that we had more energy to expel than we would on a simple cruise. Don't get me wrong, cruises are great, but look at this. Look at what I'm doing today." Bob held up a beast of a fish that I was actually afraid of even though it was out of water and almost dead. I decided right then that in the event of an apocalypse, I would be a vegetarian after all canned meats were gone. No way could I fish. Let alone kill and clean one.

"Is your story about deep-sea fishing or just fishing in general? You're from California. There's tons of fishing there, too, right?" Marge asked.

I told her that I was in Alaska covering a reality star who scored a television show, but the interview fell through. She had tons of questions about the show that I couldn't answer. She switched topics to deep-sea fishing off of the coast of California. I stared at her blankly. I named five fish in my head and only knew them because my favorite restaurant in Newport Beach had an incredible menu. I couldn't answer a single question about California fishing. I went to the beach to enjoy the water, the sun, and a cocktail or two. I knew nothing of any fishing expeditions there.

Marge and Bob told me they decided to fish in Alaska until they could no longer physically do it. She was just as excited as he was about this short day trip. My interview with them was great. They would be a draw for so many older couples thinking about doing more than just a cruise around Alaska.

Out of the eight people who chartered the boat, Marge and Bob caught the biggest halibut. I'd never, in my life, seen a fish that large before. The captain laughed at me and said it was big, but relatively, it was just average. He told me I needed to go to Anchorage in a few weeks when king salmon season started. I would see bigger fish there. Looking at the halibut that was half the size of Marge, I found it hard to believe people wrestled larger beasts from the ocean.

The water was calmer as we headed back to shore so by the time we docked, I felt human again. Lunch was still out of the question, so I hung around the fishing shacks instead, took photos, and eavesdropped on conversations. Most of the people who chartered the boats were beginners and wanted the fishing experience. When there weren't any clients, the boats went out and fished anyway. Restaurants paid top dollar for genuine Alaskan halibut. There was a lot of hard work that went into fishing and I certainly had a new appreciation for it. Never would I take my lightly grilled and seasoned halibut for granted again.

The fishing excursion was enough for a quirky and fun story. I'd include a playful approach using my seasickness with a write up of Bob and Marge as the typical tourists and their experience. It wouldn't paint me in the best light, but what did I care? Nobody I knew read *A&A*.

As much as I enjoyed Homer, I felt more at ease at the cabin in Anchorage so I decided to head back. Besides, I was excited to see Brynn again. I would go to the sanctuary this week to finish the tour and maybe steal a few more breathtaking kisses. I was excited to see Wally, too. I checked my semi-worthless GPS and it put me in Anchorage at my cabin at 5:32 p.m. Plenty of time to unwind and get cracking on the story, barring any unforeseen incidents with moose or any other of Alaska's ginormous animals.

CHAPTER TEN

How hard could it be to start a fire?" I asked no one in particular. I'd seen a thousand movies where people threw newspapers, logs, and a match on the stand inside a fireplace. I'd only ever used gas fireplaces and it wasn't hard to push a button, but it couldn't be that difficult to start a real fire.

In the hour since I'd returned to the cabin, I had fixed a quick and unfulfilling salad and was ready to sit in front of a warm fire to fight off the chilly evening. My fishing story was starting to form and I was excited to crack open my laptop. I found some balled up paper and logs stacked on the side of the fireplace. I shoved paper on the iron rack, threw some smaller logs on top, and lit it. The flames ate at the newspaper quickly, then attacked the logs. I proudly sat back to admire my handiwork. That wasn't so hard. I should've grabbed marshmallows at the grocery store to roast. When was the last time I did that?

Everything was going great until the cabin filled with smoke and, naturally, I panicked. Why wasn't the smoke going up the chimney like it was supposed to? What the fuck did I do wrong? I paced the cabin and decided to open the windows and door to air out the thickening smoke. The only thing I could think of was to douse the fire. I raced to the kitchen to fill a pan with water when I heard someone bust through the door.

"What's going on? Kennedy? Are you in here?"

"Brynn. Is that you?" I raced over to the silhouette.

"Yes. Why's there so much smoke?" she asked, covering her mouth with the sleeve of her jacket.

"I started a fire in the fireplace, but it must be broken."

She grabbed my sleeve as I headed back to the kitchen for my pot of water. "Hang on. Did you open the damper?"

There was a damper and it needed to be opened? News to me. "No." I was too terrified to even consider lying.

Brynn crawled over to the fireplace and twisted a knob on the floor. After a minute, the smoke was no longer billowing into the cabin, but enough was still pouring out the windows that it was going to take some time to air out. Brynn found me and grabbed my hand.

"Let's go outside for a bit until the smoke dissipates." She held my hand the entire time she pulled me out of the cabin. Her fingers were strong where they pressed my hand.

"Are you fucking kidding me?" I turned when I heard sirens coming onto the property. I held my head with both my hands and groaned. "Why do bad things keep happening to me?"

Brynn turned on her heel and met the fire truck before it got to the cabin. She climbed on the step and talked to the firemen. I picked the most inopportune moments to admire her uniform and its tight fit. She was so tall, she almost didn't need to use the step to talk to the driver. He immediately shut off the siren. Everybody looked at me. I was a mixture of embarrassed and angry at myself. I threw my hands up in the air like I did nothing wrong. Two of the firemen jumped down and walked over.

"So, you've never started a fire before?" The older fireman eyed me with an amused look. He elbowed his sidekick and smirked. His sidekick snickered and covered it with a cough. I looked for Brynn, but she was busy talking to Cee. "It's not that hard. It's not like it's rocket science." The sidekick laughed. My inner bitch bubbled to the surface.

"Look, Judgy McJudge, I'm sure you rock the shit out of making fires and putting them out. And I'm sure you've never made a mistake in your life because I can tell that you are perfect."

I purposely looked him up and down, slowly. I did not have a pleasant look on my face. "Not all of us are comfortable doing new things, but at least I'm giving it a try. If you came here strictly to be a dick and make me feel worse, congratulations. You've succeeded." I marched up the stairs and back into the cabin just to get away from him. I didn't care how much I coughed, I wasn't going to stand around and be insulted by him.

"Kennedy. Where are you? Come here." I turned to find Brynn standing in the doorway again.

"He's an asshole."

"Agreed, but I want you to be outside until the cabin clears completely. I told them to leave, but they want to check the place first. Let's go for a quick walk or go out on the deck." She knew exactly how to calm me. I walked over to her, my body still rigid from the exchange. She grabbed both my hands and playfully shook them back and forth until I smiled.

"Okay, but I don't want them to go through my things. They'll probably steal a pair of panties as a trophy. I don't trust them," I said.

She nodded sternly while dragging me out to the back deck. She sat me in one of the chairs. "Stay here while I let them in. I'll be in there the whole time to make sure they don't try to rummage through your stuff." She disappeared inside. The smoke was clearing so I could see her motion for the firemen to come in. Jerks. They were quick to assess it and left within a few minutes. The sidekick tipped his hat at me on his way out. I ignored him.

"Yeah, so I didn't know about the damper. I'm sorry. Is Cee going to kick me out?" I asked Brynn as she sat on the chair next to mine.

Brynn handed me my glass of wine. I loved that she thought to bring me my drink. "She's fine. There isn't any damage. A little bit of smoke smell, but that would've happened anyway even with a controlled fire." She smiled at me.

"How many times have you saved me? Three? Four? I've lost count," I said. My wine tasted smoky, but I still drank it. It calmed my frazzled nerves.

"So have I," she said playfully. She leaned over to nudge my knee. "I'll just have to check in on you every day."

My heart raced. Every day for the next two weeks sounded fantastic. "Were you checking in on me?" I wondered what she was doing here.

"No, not really. I came by to apologize for leaving so abruptly the other day at the sanctuary. And I realized I didn't have your phone number so I had to communicate the old-fashioned way. In person."

I wanted to reach over and touch her smile, but we weren't there yet. Too bad, because I could have used a Brynn Coleman kiss. "I'm glad that you did. I would've been a complete wreck without you. Cee would've kicked me out for sure." I leaned back in the chair and stared at the view, but couldn't appreciate it at the moment. I was borderline distraught.

"She understands this is all new to you and feels bad that she didn't have any instructions, so in a way you helped her. She's going to have them printed out, step-by-step, and put into each cabin to prevent future similar situations." Brynn put air quotes around similar situations.

I shuddered recalling the last half hour of my life. "Thank you. Again. So I owe you at least two dinners and my firstborn. Is that right?"

She turned toward me and pushed her hair back from her eyes. Her eyes were bright and expressive. I imagined she left a lot of broken hearts. I watched as she wiggled out of her jacket, her breasts pressed firmly against her gray button-down shirt. "Maybe even more." She lifted her eyebrow at me.

I grinned. "You're right." Those were words I never said in my other life. I was always stubborn and headstrong, even when I was wrong. Yet, I had no desire to fake anything with Brynn. She saw the real me, bare bones, at several low points, and hadn't run away. "I owe you whatever you want."

Brynn could have said anything right then, but instead she leaned forward and kissed me again. It was soft and sweet and I craved more when she pulled away. I was so ready for her to take control of us and maybe not throw me down, but at least make a move. I wanted to know what her body on top of mine felt like. Most of my casual encounters were women about my size and the sex was fast and hard. Brynn was taller and stronger than any woman I had ever kissed. I wanted her to touch me everywhere, slowly. I pulled her to me and kissed her with the passion and desire I felt. Maybe the adrenaline of the moment and watching her take control of the situation turned me on, but I was not going to settle for just a sweet kiss.

Her mouth was so warm on mine. Her tongue darted out to lick my bottom lip, then my top one. She was teasing me. Just when I was ready to growl in frustration, she slipped her tongue inside of my mouth, slowly, deeply. I whimpered in submission. She pulled me to my feet as she stood up, and continued to kiss me as her strong hands dropped to my hips. I moved into her, my body fully pressed against hers. I felt her stiffen and take a step back.

"Um, so I should probably go check on the fire," she said when she broke our kiss.

We both stood there panting. I took a deep breath and closed my eyes. She was saying no to me. Nobody was this chivalrous. She was attracted to me. Nobody could kiss like that and not feel something, anything. I wasn't going to beg though. I straightened my clothes and nodded at her.

She walked in and headed straight for the fire. It was still burning, but completely under control, unlike my libido. Brynn took a poker and stirred the logs. Most of the smoke was gone so I closed the door, but left the windows open. I shivered.

"You should put a sweater on or come over here to the fire," she said quietly.

I didn't want to be that close to her for fear of making a fool of myself. Again. I headed to the loft and found a sweater in the dresser. I didn't have a lot of clothes and decided I needed to pick up a few more things. I would get sick of myself after two more weeks of the same two sweaters, boring sweatshirts, and jeans. Even though I was mad at Brynn, I was determined to at least look my best around her from now on.

"Have you eaten tonight or do you want me to fix you a salad?" I leaned over the railing so that she could hear me better. Her eyes were dark when they met mine. She was turned on. Even if she didn't touch me the way I wanted her to, the desire was there. I headed back to the dresser and discreetly removed my bra. If she wasn't going to cooperate with me, I wasn't going to play fair.

"I grabbed something on the way over. I really did just want to check on you," she said. She averted her eyes when I climbed down the ladder and headed for her. No way was Brynn shy.

"Brynn Coleman," I said. She looked at me, a guilty expression on her face. I wondered what was on her mind. "Would you like my phone number?"

She laughed and opened her contacts on her phone. "Please." She handed it to me.

I typed in my information and even though I was tempted to send a message to myself so that I had her number, I decided to wait. I didn't want to seem desperate. I wanted her to make any and all moves from here on out. "Now, you can just call me if you want to check on me. Less wear and tear on the car. Less gas. I promise to always answer unless I'm in the shower, asleep, or kidnapped. Deal?"

"Good. I guess now that things are quiet here, I should go." She didn't sound like she wanted to leave.

"How's Wally doing?" I asked when she reached out for the doorknob. I wanted her to stay for a bit longer. Wally was a viable excuse.

"Did you stay and visit with him after I left the other day?" Brynn asked.

"I didn't stay long after you left. I felt out of place. It's better with you as my tour guide. Hopefully we can reschedule if there's more to see." If I was going to write about the sanctuary, I'd need to get a better feel for it.

"What's your weekend like? I have it off and we can finish the tour without interruptions." I liked the way she leaned against the doorframe, her lithe body relaxed, her arms crossed, and her lips full of promise.

"I can make some time." My schedule was clear, but I didn't want to seem anxious. I already threw myself at her once. "I spent yesterday and most of today in Homer. It's such a cute town."

"Did you go out on a fishing boat?" she asked. She took a step toward me and ran her finger on the counter. She wanted to stay, but for some reason, she was afraid to. I took a step closer to her.

"It was kind of a disaster for me, but great for the story."

She grinned. "A little too much, huh? Sometimes the water can get rough." She shrugged and leaned her elbows on the counter.

The cool air from the open windows made me shiver. I felt my nipples harden and took a step backward. The fire only made my chill bumps worse. I didn't look because I knew they were at attention and my blouse and thin sweater did little to hide them. Even though I was slim, I had decent size breasts. Brynn had the decency to maintain eye contact and I wondered if her peripheral vision was good. I wanted her to see me. I wanted her to notice.

"Listen. I talked to my boss yesterday and threw out the idea of writing a feature story on the sanctuary instead of nine thousand pages on fishing. She liked the idea. It could bring more visitors or even donations. Would you and your staff be willing to work with me?" I exaggerated the page count for fun, and mentally cringed as I waited for her answer. Brynn was a private person and was staying low key for a reason. I didn't want to expose her if her goal was to hide out in Alaska.

Her gray eyes, full of swirling emotions, met mine. "I think that's a great idea. I know everybody would love to talk to you. That means good press, good exposure. Grants and government funding only stretch so far."

"Oh, good. I'm so excited. It's such a great place. You've done an excellent job there."

She blushed and brushed her hair out of her eyes. "We all do good work, but thank you." It was nice to see her eyes light up and a genuine smile on her face. She was so pretty when she relaxed. I wanted her to stay.

"Do you want to stay and have a glass of wine? I still need to thank you for coming to my rescue again." I realized the implication of my offer when Brynn stilled her movements. "And to celebrate the article. I mean, it's just a simple glass of wine. I can stand here, you can stand there. We'll have a nice, safe counter between us. What do you say?" I knew the answer was no when I saw her shoulders droop ever so slightly. I sighed.

"I need to get home. But thank you. Some other time, okay?"

"Sure." I nodded and walked around to open the door for her.

"I have your number, Kennedy Wells. And I'm not afraid to use it. Don't forget to make sure the fire's out before you go to sleep."

She walked by me and reached out to briefly touch my arm. It was amazing that I could feel her heat from just a simple touch.

"I'll see you soon." I closed the door and walked over to the fire. I poked it like I knew what I was doing, but I just wasn't excited about it anymore. Brynn confused me. I wasn't used to back and forth like high school. Maybe this was how the real world dated. I couldn't remember my last date. It was way before Nikki Toles wreaked havoc on my life. I thought hard and drew a blank. I couldn't remember anything. I realized that I hadn't been in a real relationship since college. That was depressing. Alaska was making me do something I hadn't done in a really long time. Reflect.

Chapter Eleven

Ready to pick up where we left off?" Brynn leaned out of the truck window and I had to stop for a moment to absorb the differences in her. She looked so relaxed and happy. "It's going to be a beautiful day."

Wally poked his head up from her lap and I squealed. "Wally. How are you?" I leaned into the window and scratched his little ear. I was in Brynn's personal space and I didn't care.

"Good morning, Kennedy."

I turned to Brynn and smiled. "Good morning." I kept eye contact with Brynn as I walked to the passenger side. Wally greeted me at the door. "Hello, my prince." I reached in to pet his chest and he gently grabbed my hand.

"Well, I hate to admit that I'm kind of jealous of the attention," Brynn said.

I stood there not knowing if I should flirt back or roll my eyes at her. I climbed into the truck and buckled in before I answered. "I don't even know what to say to that." Surely she remembered when I pressed my entire body against her just two nights ago. She ignored my statement.

"So today we're going to the north end of the sanctuary where you will see more animals. I figure we can drop Wally off first and see what's going on with Tina. She has a few animals I think you will like to meet. That way you get a better idea of what we do."

"My camera's charged and ready," I said. Wally stood on my lap and looked out the windshield. Erin would never believe this. I snapped a selfie of us and sent it to her.

"Let's go." Brynn spent the drive time telling me more about Alaska and her career. I found it interesting how easily she slipped into this ranger role. It started when her dog got hurt after a fight with a coyote only six months after she moved to Anchorage. Brynn took both her dog and the coyote to the closest vet which happened to be Tina's private practice. Her practice was for domestic animals, but she knew enough about wild ones to treat them as well. "Honestly I only wrestled with the coyote and took him to Tina because I wanted to know if he had rabies. Besides, Blackie got ahold of him pretty good and he needed stitches, too."

"You had both animals in the car?" I couldn't believe she would take such a risk.

"Sort of. It was a highly stressful situation. Blackie was in the front seat next to me and the coyote was in the bed of my truck in a cage. Tina stitched both up and brought the coyote here. She thought he might have been a pet at one time or somewhat domesticated based on how well he took to her."

"How did you not get bitten? That's crazy."

"I did the blanket trick. Back then, I didn't realize everything that could've gone wrong. I'm better educated at capturing animals now." Brynn turned into the parking lot and I smiled when Wally became animated.

"Look at this little guy. He knows his home away from home," I said. I waited for Brynn to get out of the truck and reach for Wally before I opened the door. Knowing my luck, I would open the door and Wally would scamper off.

I followed Brynn into the animal hospital behind the Welcoming Center after securing Wally in Brynn's office. The hospital was at least twice the size of the center with large, spacious rooms for the vets to perform all kinds of treatments. Several rooms had doors that led to outdoor pens. I started snapping photos before I even thought about asking questions. There were several large birds, beautiful foxes, a lynx, two mountain goats, and even a small aquarium for water animals. The accommodations were chilly so I was glad Brynn handed me a jacket when we arrived. My new sweater wasn't warm enough. Tina was working on a bird who was either dead or knocked out. I turned to Brynn. "Is Owlie still here?"

She nodded and we quietly made our way over to another room where the animals had larger cages and more space to move around. "He seems to be good to go. On Monday, I'm going to release him near Mrs. Wright's place. We aren't quite sure where he came from since we don't see a lot of them. That seems to be the best idea."

I snapped a few photos of him and other animals awaiting release. This place was amazing. It must cost a fortune to maintain. "Can I go with you when you do? I want to see him fly away." And I wanted to spend more time with Brynn. I had about two weeks left, but I was going to be busy most of next week researching and interviewing for my article. That left my time with Brynn and any opportunity for something more than kissing limited. I was going to stretch our time as long as I could.

"Sure. I know you have a busy schedule coming up though. There will be so much going on, you won't know which way to turn."

"Is fishing that much of a draw?"

"It's amazing how popular it is. I'll take you to a place where you can see the bears fishing. They are incredibly graceful and quick." Brynn opened the door and ushered me back inside to visit with Tina. She was still working on the bird.

"Please tell me that bird's not dead." Why would Brynn bring me to an animal autopsy?

Tina was hunched over a bird under a bright lamp. A bright orange and yellow beak stood out against a white, deflated breast. His wings, so black they shone blue under the light, were carefully outstretched. "No, I'm just fixing a tear he has in his wing. Then I'll tag him and put him in recovery. He'll be fine in a couple of days."

"Phew. I was worried. He looks dead." I moved closer and stared at his features. "What is he? He's beautiful."

"Tina, this is Kennedy. She's here from California to do a story on the sanctuary. We're just doing a quick tour of the center."

"Hi, Kennedy. I've already heard so much about you," she said. Her smile couldn't have been any larger.

I turned to Brynn. "She knows?"

Brynn had the audacity to blush. "Well, it was a hard story not to share," she said.

"Yeah, Alaska hasn't been kind to me. At least Brynn was able to come to my rescue several times. We're bound by my many misfortunes," I said.

"Brynn's a great woman to have in your court. And don't feel bad about everything that's happened. Trust me, worse things have happened here." She glanced at Brynn. "Remember when that couple hit not one, but two elk?" She turned back to me. "It was the craziest thing. They hit one elk and, after determining their RV was drivable, headed back out on the road and hit another one about fifty feet away. That was also on their first day, so don't beat yourself up so much."

"That makes me feel a teensy bit better. Thanks." I was afraid to ask what happened to the elk so I didn't. In my head, they survived. "Can I take a photo of him? He's quite beautiful." I snapped a few of Tina stitching him up after she agreed.

"He's a tufted puffin. They are actually mean as hell and not friendly," Tina said.

"Ready to see some of the larger animals?" Brynn asked. The excitement on her face was undeniable. She loved her job. We went back to the truck and headed onto the highway. "We'll be able to see a lot of goats and sheep since we're headed toward the mountains."

We spent the rest of the morning at the north end where I saw mountain goats and Dall sheep. Brynn explained that they set two free, but the sheep were determined to stay at the sanctuary. Every morning, the rangers would find them back near the north entrance with their entire family in tow, so they just decided to keep them even though they were more than capable of surviving anywhere. One charged me when I got too close to the cliff they were climbing. I was surprised at how sure-footed they all were, including the babies.

"How about some lunch? I'm starving," Brynn said.

I nodded. "It's amazing how hungry I always am since I got here," I said. My clothes still fit, but I was nervous. Nobody could eat as much butter as I had and not pack on some fluff.

"I live just over there." Brynn pointed to a dirt road that was barely visible from the road.

"Can I see your place?" I blurted out before I even had a chance to mind my manners.

"Ah, sure. I can't guarantee that it's clean, but we can stop for a minute." She seemed nervous. Crap. That was rude, but I didn't know how to take it back. She turned on the road and was quiet as we drove up the narrow gravel driveway. A modest-size log and stone cabin with a wraparound porch came into view once we cleared the hill.

"Brynn. Is that your house? It's beautiful." I slid out of the truck and looked around. A matching barn sat behind and to the right of it. "How much land do you have here?"

"About five acres." She shrugged. "It's private enough, but just off of the main road."

"Can we go inside, or no?" I was halfway up the stairs already.

"Sure." She leaned past me to unlock the door. I didn't move. I liked it when she was close to me. She smelled like cedar and sage. I leaned closer. She cleared her throat and pushed the door open. "Come on in." Her eyes dropped down to my lips. I brushed by her, my fingers grazing her stomach on purpose, but I pretended it was an accident.

"This place is gorgeous, Brynn. How old is it?"

"We finished construction on it about eight months ago."

I could tell she was proud. "You built this yourself?"

"I helped, but no, a friend of mine owns a construction company and gave me a really good deal."

I nodded and wondered what that was like. Nicety wasn't a thing where I was from without a price. "Will you give me a tour?" I was as excited as I was the other day when the herd of bison walked by us.

"Of course."

The open floor plan was a surprise. I expected a series of rooms decorated with animal heads and antique rifles. From the doorway, I could see past the kitchen with gleaming new appliances, through the dining area with a long, polished table and two benches that easily seated twelve guests, all the way to the sitting area with a couch and two overstuffed chairs. The fireplace was gorgeous and even though the décor was sparse, it was a lovely home.

When we got to her bedroom, I gasped. It was so different. She had put up drywall over the logs and painted the room so it lost the rustic feel the rest of the house had. A giant stone fireplace opposite her four-poster bed automatically gave the bedroom a warm feeling.

"I would never leave this room, Brynn." A rolltop desk sat in the corner opposite a chaise lounge. A tiny bed sat on the floor beside the bed. I laughed and pointed. She walked over to see what I saw. "Do you really expect me to believe that Wally sleeps there and not curled up beside you?" I leaned over and playfully poked her side. She squealed and backed away.

"Oh, you don't want to do that." She lifted my hands off her body.

"Yes, I do," I said, and moved closer. "Who knew that the big, bad butch was so ticklish?" I pushed myself so that I was once again flush against her hard body.

Her breathing changed. Her eyes darkened. For a moment, I was nervous. Maybe I pushed her too far. She didn't move. I leaned forward and kissed her. When she released my hands, I looped them behind her neck and deepened the kiss. I felt her hands find my waist as she pushed me back against the bed. She didn't let me fall, but held me as we both tumbled onto the bed. I moaned when I felt her body rest between my legs. I bucked against her and ran my hands down her back until I found her belt. I pulled her into me and gasped when her belt buckle hit my swollen clit through my jeans. I felt the warmth of her fingertips on my bare stomach when she slipped her hand underneath my sweater. I couldn't stop the chills that raced across my body and I didn't want to. I wanted to feel the power in her caress. She dug her fingers into my waist and started grinding herself into me. I was so ready to come that I growled when I felt her pull away from me. "No, Brynn. Please don't. Don't pull away from me."

"I'm sorry. I…I shouldn't have done that," she said and crawled off of me.

I pushed my sweater down and covered my eyes with the crook of my arm. I was embarrassed and pissed. My body was on fire and my temper was several degrees higher than that. I heard her pace the bedroom, but I refused to look at her. What the fuck was happening here? One minute her hands were all over me, the next she couldn't get away from me fast enough. After about thirty seconds of feeling sorry for myself, I sat up. Brynn was leaning against her chaise, her arms crossed, her eyes intently on me.

"Why? Why do you keep pulling away from me?" I ran my hands through my hair and tried hard to act normal, but I was shaking. I didn't want to stand just yet. I couldn't let her see how much her rejection bothered me. Again.

She resumed her pacing. "It's not you. I know that sounds completely ridiculous. But I just don't think this is a good move. I mean, you aren't here for very long and I don't do well at these kinds of things," she said.

"What does that mean exactly?" I stood and walked over to her. She averted her eyes. "Seriously. What do you mean by these kinds of things?"

"Kennedy, I'm not great at this," she said as if I knew what she meant.

"Not good at this? Like kissing? Making out? Sex? Exactly what aren't you good at?" I was mad and I didn't want to think about why.

"All of it. I don't want to open myself up to this and then you leave in two weeks. I tend to put a lot of emotion into connecting with another woman and I don't want either of us to get hurt." She walked around me, but stayed close. "Somebody a lot like you hurt me a long time ago and it took me a long time to get past it."

I walked over to her and carefully touched her arm. "I'm not her. I'm sorry you got hurt, but that's not my intent. I like you, Brynn. You are strong and sweet and you make me feel…" I paused and searched for the right word. "Protected. You make me feel safe." Brynn hung her head. I could tell she struggled with her own demons. I stepped back away from her. This wasn't going to happen no matter how much I wanted it. "Can you please take me to my cabin?" I didn't want to cry in front of her. What was happening to me? Back home, I didn't care if a woman said no to me. Well, actually, I couldn't remember the last time one did. She nodded and I walked out of the bedroom in front of her. "You do have a nice place," I said and granted myself one last quick look on my way out the front door. I doubted that I would ever see it again.

Chapter Twelve

"Thanks for inviting me over. It's nice having new friends," I said. I toasted Mandy and her wife, Lisa, before we started our dinner of smoked salmon. I was excited to try genuine fresh Alaska salmon and Lisa promised me it would be the best I ever tasted.

"Thank you for taking time out of your schedule to have dinner with us. Mandy said you were working on a big spread for *Antlers & Anglers* magazine. We love tourists here. They support all of the local businesses," Lisa said. She clinked her glass with mine and then with Mandy. The look they shared was sweet and tender and I felt guilty for witnessing it. Ten years and they still shared passion. I loved it and hated it at the same time. I doubted I would ever find that for myself. I was too set in my ways at thirty-one.

"Hopefully I'll get it right and send some people your way," I said. I took my first bite of the salmon and moaned as it practically melted in my mouth. "I found heaven in Alaska." Fresh fish was so light and tasty and void of the sharpness that a lot of fish dishes had. It flaked right off my fork. I also tried not to think that just one hour ago, this fish was alive and happily swimming in the ocean.

"You've been here about a week, right?" At my nod, Lisa continued. "Plenty of time to try everything."

"I tried a halibut burger and a salmon burger earlier in the week. Both were delicious," I said. I felt a pang of sadness thinking about Brynn. I thought about her more than I should. I hadn't talked to her since she dropped me off at my cabin yesterday afternoon. I cringed thinking about our exchange in her bedroom. Not one of my finest moments.

"From Buster's?" Mandy asked.

"I honestly don't know. I met a ranger from the Alaskan Wildlife Rescue. She brought me dinner last week after I had an incident hiking."

"She probably got them from Buster's. Everybody goes there for great burgers," Mandy said.

Lisa nodded. "Which ranger was it? We know some of the rangers stationed at the Sanctuary."

"Brynn Coleman. Do you know her?" Mandy and Lisa exchanged a look. I wondered what that was about, but I played it off instead. I was good at extracting information when the time was right.

"Yeah, we know Brynn. She's great. How did you meet her?" Mandy asked.

I groaned. I didn't want more of Alaska to know that story so I downplayed it. "I had kind of a run in with a moose. Brynn showed up and did her moose whisperer magic and got it to leave me alone." I left out the part about the car getting squished and me near tears over the entire incident.

"That sounds like Brynn." Mandy smiled. "She's so good with animals. Working at the sanctuary's truly the best job for her. Most of the time, it's rewarding, but I know it's so hard for her when she has to put an animal down. I can't even imagine what she goes through."

I never thought about that. That was probably why she disappeared off of my radar for almost two days after the first partial tour of the sanctuary. When she got the call, she tensed immediately and I felt her pull away as she steeled herself against what was to come. "I couldn't do it. I'm not a super huge animal fan, but still. That has to be the hardest thing."

"She's so emotional, too, even though she tries hard to hide it," Mandy said. I cocked my head with interest. That was news to me.

"Do you know her well?" I asked. They shared another look. "Okay, I know she's a lesbian."

"Okay, phew. We didn't want to out her if she hadn't said anything yet." Mandy said.

I wasn't going to share the fact that we'd kissed several times and I'd felt her gloriously tall and strong body on top of mine. Or that I'd all but begged her to have sex with me. Nope. I was going to go to my grave with that embarrassing information.

"We've known Brynn about five years or so. We've seen her in some of the clubs and we play on the same softball team. She's a bit standoffish, but super nice and a great athlete." Mandy refilled our wineglasses.

"I can't even tell you how many times she has saved me this past week. The moose, my boots, the fire." I shook my head at all of my mishaps.

"Wow. So you really do know Brynn. She keeps to herself most days. She must like you," Lisa said.

"She's been very helpful, like Mandy, on getting information for my articles. It'll be hard to narrow down the sanctuary story to ten pages and photos. My boss is crazy if she thinks she'll be able to sum up the sanctuary with so few photos. Maybe I should ask Brynn to be less informative." I chuckled.

"Brynn's the first one to help someone. Always. We just wish she would find somebody up here," Mandy said.

Thank God I wasn't hitting on somebody who was taken, although it didn't make me feel any better. It just meant that Brynn wasn't interested in me and that stung.

"Is the queer population large here in Alaska? Are you comfortable being out?" I couldn't imagine my life as anything but out. California was so open, it never crossed my mind to hide my sexuality.

"I don't think Alaska has a large queer population. I think it falls right in the middle of the spectrum. There aren't a lot of people here, but the percentages are about the same as anywhere else. There are moments when we haven't felt safe, but for the most part, people are accepting. When they finally legalized gay marriage, we ran to the courthouse and got married as soon as we could," Lisa said.

I swore if I wasn't there, they would've had sex right on the table based on the smoldering look they shared. I wanted to steer the conversation back to Brynn, but I was having a hard time coming up with an appropriate segue without being obvious.

"That's sweet. I'm sure it's hard to meet someone here in Alaska. You are kind of separated from the rest of the states. But Brynn's adorable. I'm sure she'll find somebody soon," I said.

Mandy took the bait. "I just wish it was sooner than later."

I tried not to smile. "Did she have bad luck in the past?"

"It took forever for her to get involved in any social activities or even hit the bars. She's dated a few women, but nothing serious. I think she's waiting for the right woman to come along, but it's not as if Alaska's brimming with available lesbians. She would do so well in the lower forty-eight. Tall, gorgeous, athletic. You should take her back to California with you, Kennedy," Mandy said.

I nodded, surprisingly jealous at the thought of Brynn in my social circle, dating women I knew. "Well, other than not having a partner, Alaska seems like the perfect place for her."

"Agreed. We should have her over for dinner again. It's been too long." Lisa turned to Mandy. "Next time you see her, invite her." Mandy nodded. I guess the Brynn conversation was over. The only information I'd gathered that evening was that she wasn't dating anyone else, but she clearly wasn't interested in me.

Chapter Thirteen

I decided to branch out further than Anchorage because I was getting antsy. Brynn could be anywhere and I didn't want to accidentally run into her. I did, but I didn't. I wanted it to be on my terms. I grabbed one of the maps she gave me the first time we met and headed out with my backpack, the ridiculous bear spray, and a walking stick. There were several streams and lakes within an hour's drive and I wanted to get some photos of popular places. I worked on the fishing story the night before and got quite a bit done. It was still boring, but I had faith that I would come up with a fun twist.

I parked in a gravel lot and gave a sigh of relief when I saw two other trucks, both with trailers hitched to them. I'd seen this a lot already. It meant I would not be alone out here. I hoped that was good news, not something I had to worry about. Most of the people I'd met in Alaska were friendly, but I knew to always have my guard up. I grabbed my stuff, tightened my boots, and picked a trail. All of them led to the wide fishing stream, just at different places.

The hike I chose was a mile and a half long. I approached it with gusto and prayed that I wouldn't encounter anything larger than a squirrel. When I reached the stream, I stopped and soaked in my surroundings. It was so lovely and virtually untouched by civilization. The water was crystal clear, unlike any I'd ever seen before. Tan, gray, pink, and white rocks dotted the bed several feet down. I smiled at the tiny fish darting around the stones.

I snapped several photos and walked upstream until I saw a doe, or elk, or some deer-like creature drinking peacefully. She was majestic. I took a few photos of her close up, and zoomed out so I got the stream and the mountains. It was a beautifully balanced photo and I loved everything about it. When I heard the gunshot and saw the doe drop, I gasped.

I instinctively crouched to hide. I had no idea what was going on. I was unsure of hunting around the area and I was wearing a brown jacket. I didn't want to be mistaken for a deer. I wished I could remember what Brynn told me about hunting season. This was part of a national park system, I thought, and only the rangers thinned out the herd. Why would hunters be here when it was obviously a place for tourists with trails and markers? I didn't stand up and identify myself when they surrounded their kill. One of the hunters pulled out a knife and I looked away. I didn't want to see what he was doing.

"Really, Randy? Why did you shoot it? It's not like we'll get anything for her. Now we're going to have to take her with us." One of the hunters slapped his hat against his leg in frustration.

"Yeah, well, you can thank me later when you're eating caribou burgers," he said.

None of them had safety orange on. From the looks of it, I had just witnessed poaching. I slowly scooted to my left so I would be covered by more underbrush and took photos of the three hunters that were standing around the doe. Through the lens, they all looked similar; unkempt beards, brown clothing, and tall boots. They dragged the carcass to a clearing off to the left.

"Go get the truck." There was no way they were going to get one of the trucks through these woods.

I heard the names Randy and Jim, but the third man was never identified. I didn't move an inch. All of this screamed danger and I was smack dab in the middle of it. My legs ached from being bent at an awkward angle. My neck was cramped. I was hungry and I had to go to the bathroom. I wanted to cry. I wanted Brynn. I pulled my phone out of my pocket but realized she had my number, but I didn't have hers. Son of a bitch. I should've sent myself a text from her phone when she had me fill out my contact information. I considered calling 9-1-1, but the response I'd gotten before didn't give me much confidence.

I slowly moved around and stretched out my legs so they were flat on the ground. I was quiet, careful not to attract their attention. It would be a while until the third returned. The parking lot was over a mile away. I slowly wiggled my legs, one at a time, to ensure that I still had blood flow and feelings. My back was killing me because I was hunched over. I was miserable.

"What was that?" One of them asked.

Fuck. Did I make a noise? Just my luck, some critter scurried right outside of the brush I was hiding behind. I bit my hand to keep from screaming out. I grabbed a rock with my other hand so I could bash its head in if it tried to make a meal out of me. I didn't know what was worse—getting killed by poachers, or eaten alive by a bear. A rodent that looked like a guinea pig on steroids ran across my leg and I muffled my yell. Thankfully, he shot out past me and left my hiding place. I heard the guys laugh at it.

"You're so on edge, Jim."

"Hey, this isn't something we do this close to the road, let alone in broad daylight." Poaching confirmed.

They stopped talking when the hum of an engine approached. No way did that trailer get in this deep. I peeked out. They had an off-road four-wheeler with a flat, steel trailer on wheels. The driver jumped out and walked over to the other two.

"We have a problem. There's another car in the parking lot. Somebody's here."

Just when I thought they were five minutes away from leaving and I thought I was going to get out of this unscathed.

"Well, let's get this back to the camper and take a look around." I shrank even lower. I watched as they loaded the body and put a tarp over it. I kept my eye on them until they drove out of sight. The second they disappeared, I jumped up and ignored all the aches and pains in my body and ran as fast as I could the other way. I was hoping I could get to the parking lot about the time they turned around to look for me. I'd hide there until I felt like I could make a clean dash to the car.

I thanked my personal trainer back home for always kicking my ass. Because of him, I was able to run at a steady pace. I stopped to load my camera into my backpack because it was too tight around my neck and bumped against my ribs. When I approached the parking lot, I slowed down and hid behind a large trail marking boulder. They were done loading the carcass into the trailer and were pushing the four-wheeler into the other one. They would start searching for me next.

Since my camera was packed away, I took my cell phone out and snapped a few photos of the trucks and even got a few faces. I was too far away to make out facial details, or license plates, but I was closer than I was before. When they locked up, I slid down the back of the rock and prayed they would not come this way. The main guy barked out orders and I shivered when the other two responded. One was headed in my direction. The only choice I had was to show myself. Running away would be a dead giveaway. I did the only thing I could think of. I took off my boot and sock and started crying.

"I found someone." The largest man I could imagine looked at me. His beard was brown on the verge of gray, and his eyes were squinting so much that I couldn't tell the color. He looked like he had no idea what to do with me.

I reacted the only way I knew how in Alaska. Damsel in distress. The past week had given me ample practice. Judging by the way he held himself and the menacing way he looked me over, I was screwed. I was going to have to put on the performance of a lifetime.

"Oh, my God. I'm so glad you're here. I didn't know someone was on the trail. Can you help me back to my car? Look at my blisters." I stopped to sob for a moment. "I don't even know how

I managed to get this far." I held my hand out for him to grab, loathing myself for having to stoop to this level.

He pulled me up, almost into his chest, and I had to stop myself from recoiling. I had to pretend he was just some guy I happened to run into in the middle of nowhere. He walked me toward the other two, who were standing right by my car. I hobbled the best I could and pretended I was in a lot of pain. My blisters still looked bad and I hoped they would believe me.

"What are you doing out here?" The obvious guy in charge crossed his arms and massaged his beard with his right hand as he waited for my answer.

"I was taking a walk and decided to come back to my car because my blisters started hurting." All three looked at my foot. It was covered in dust, but the blisters were evident.

"How long have you been here?" he asked.

"Not long because I didn't notice her car until this last time." The one whose name I think was Randy said. The other one smacked him.

"He's right. I just got here. I thought I could walk today, but I overestimated it. Is this a good trail though? I have a ton of trail maps that the hotel gave me when I got here and this wasn't too far out of my way." I was rambling and doing everything I could to throw them off. I placed my boot on the hood of my car while I slid my sock on.

"What's in your backpack?" The leader asked. I tried to look nonchalant. I hope it didn't translate into fear.

"Protein bars, water, and my camera. Oh, and extra socks. Why?" I dropped my boot onto the ground and slipped into it carefully. I had to keep the ruse of painful blisters going.

"What are you taking pictures of? Mind if we look?" The look in his eye told me I didn't have a choice.

"Yes, I mind." I tried to act inconvenienced. He roughly grabbed my backpack almost causing me to fall. His strength scared me. "Are you kidding me? You can't accost me like this and demand to go through my things. I have rights," I said. All three laughed.

"Who knows how to turn this thing on?" He held my camera like it was a toy. Even though I didn't pay the thousands of dollars it was worth, my company did. I didn't want to have to file another personal property claim with our insurance company for it.

"Careful with that." I stretched for it and he held it out of my reach as if playing a game of keep away.

"Not until I see what's on this. Turn it on for me." He thrust it back at me and waited.

I almost cried tears of joy when two cars full of hikers pulled into the parking lot and parked next to me. I took that opportunity to step away from the poachers and go around to the passenger side of my SUV. Thankfully, my car keys were in my jacket pocket. I jumped in and scooted over to the driver's side. I barely looked at the three men as I pulled away. I hit the highway and sped as fast as I could.

I had no idea who to call other than Brynn and I didn't even have her number. I thought about calling the sanctuary for her, but I was panicked and I needed to calm down. I could have called the police, but I didn't know what to report. Plus with their fresh kill, I'm sure they wanted to get away from there as soon as possible. I was certain they were poaching, but maybe I was wrong about hunting season. Maybe hunters didn't wear safety orange here. Brynn mentioned that hunting hadn't improved much since the eighteen hundreds and the laws constantly changed based on politicians in office. I was confused and angry, and I just wanted to go home. I was done with Alaska. Every day here was just bad. Those men were jerks. For what they were doing, for what they did. I was pissed that they had my bag, but at least there wasn't anything important in it. Just my food and water. I was pretty sure I took off my luggage tag when I unpacked. I'd have to check when I got back to my cabin. Fuck. My cabin key with the name of Cee's cabins beautifully etched on a wooden key chain was in the backpack.

CHAPTER FOURTEEN

"Cee, is there any way you can call Brynn for me?" By the time I was back at the cabins, I was a complete wreck. I drove ten miles over the speed limit with my eyes glued to the rearview mirror the entire time. "And I'm so sorry, but I lost my key. Can I get another one? You can charge me for it."

"What happened to you?" Cee jumped up and came around the desk to inspect me. My boot was barely on, bits and pieces of leaves and twigs were tangled in my hair, and I had torn my jeans at the knee.

"I was at the wrong place at the wrong time," I said.

She grabbed her phone from the desk and dialed Brynn. "Hi, there. What are you doing?" There was a pause as Cee allowed Brynn the opportunity to answer before hitting her with my news. "I have somebody here who would like to talk to you." She handed the phone to me. I was so nervous, I dropped it on the counter.

"Crap. I'm sorry Cee." I picked it up and sighed. "Brynn. It's Kennedy. I'm sorry to bother you, but I really need to talk to you. Can you come by when you're off duty?"

Cee grabbed the phone from me. "Brynn, you probably should get here sooner rather than later." I heard concern in Brynn's voice when she told Cee she would be right over.

"You didn't have to scare her. I don't want her to get hurt driving here," I said.

Cee pointed to a chair. "Go sit. She'll be here in twenty minutes."

I didn't feel like being alone so I did what she told me. Cee made me hot tea. I wasn't cold, but the heat was comforting when I curved my hands around the mug and held it close. Brynn was at Cee's cabin in fifteen minutes. The look she gave me when she saw me made my heart stop. It was fierce and protective and made me want to cry.

"What happened?" she asked. She sat on the coffee table directly in front of me. She was completely in my personal space and as much as I wanted to sink into her and feel her warmth envelop me, I stayed strong, leaned back, and told her my story.

"You shouldn't go anywhere alone ever." Her tone was a mix of panic and barely controlled anger. She was upset, but not at me.

"It was a clearly marked path. I thought it was okay." I didn't recognize my own voice. I sounded defeated and tired.

"Are you okay?" She reached out toward me, then drew her hand back.

"A few bruises here and there, I'm sure, but I'm fine. I got away before anything happened," I said. She stood and started pacing. "There's worse news." She stopped pacing and stared at me.

"Tell me."

"They took my bag that had my cabin key in it. And it might have my luggage tag with my name on it. I don't know if I took it off, but they definitely know where I'm staying." I cringed.

Brynn swore under her breath, shook her head, and walked outside. The screen door smacked loudly into place after she pushed through it. I sat there, not knowing what to do. I looked at Cee who shrugged at me. I decided to go after Brynn because I wasn't sure what my next move should be. I needed her advice. She opened the door before I had a chance to grab the handle and just stopped short of crashing into me.

"You're staying with me," she said. Her voice was firm and her gaze hard.

"Excuse me?" Granted, the idea wasn't bad, but I wasn't used to being bossed around by anyone.

"It's not safe for you here." She looked over at Cee. "You need to be careful, too, and have John and the dogs close by because we don't know what these people are capable of. They know about Kennedy and they know she's here." Brynn put her hands on my elbows and looked at me. Her gray eyes were almost black. She was serious. "I want you to stay with me until we get this sorted out. Poaching's a serious crime and these guys know that you've seen their faces, their trucks, and probably have pictures of them. The best place for you to be is right next to me. I can keep an eye on you twenty-four seven." She nodded once, insinuating that the decision was made.

My feminist hackles didn't like her Neanderthal grunts and commands, but I also trusted her and those guys were scary so I caved. I turned to Cee. "I'm so sorry, Cee. I hope they don't cause any trouble for you."

"Don't worry about me. We'll be fine here." She waved it off like three angry, burly poachers on her property wasn't a concern. "I have guns everywhere and I'm not afraid to use them." I never expected words like that to fit in my life. If someone had said that to me two weeks before, I would have packed it up for the season and headed somewhere far away from Alaska.

"Let's get your stuff together. And let's get rid of your car," Brynn said.

"Like dump it?" There was no way my company would pay for a total loss. I got lucky the first time that it wasn't on their dime.

Brynn laughed for the first time since she arrived. "No. I mean, let's turn it in. I would advise against renting from the same place. That way, if these guys start sniffing around and see that you aren't here and your rental car's back, they'll think you went home. They won't chase you there."

"Well, can't they just walk the two steps to the other car counter and ask if Kennedy Wells rented a car from them?" I wasn't trying to be a snob, but it wasn't like there were a ton of car rental options.

"Okay, new plan. We'll drop off your car and I'll loan you one of mine," Brynn said.

I liked that idea even less. After our uncomfortable encounter the other day, I didn't want to feel like I owed her any more than I already did. "No, it's okay. I'll just go to a different place." Out of the corner of my eye, I saw Brynn's lips move as she silently counted to ten. Great. I infuriated her. "And I can just go to a hotel. Thanks for the offer, but I think I'll be fine." I threw that in because I didn't want Brynn to know that I wanted her protection. My pride wouldn't allow it, even though she had helped me countless times.

"We need to hurry and get you out of here. We can deal with the location when we're on the road, okay?" She turned to me, her eyes dark and angry. I nodded and winced. She held the door for me and followed me up the path to my cabin. Not a word was spoken. "I'll wait out here while you pack up," she said.

I shrugged my shoulders like a child. "Fine. Whatever you want." I was in a hurry to get out of there so I packed and did a final walkthrough in under ten minutes.

Brynn took the luggage out to her Jeep. I looked around the cabin before I shut the door and smiled at all of the memories. Seeing thousands of stars at night, the fading ribbons of the aurora borealis, Wally playing with an empty box and making himself comfortable here, Brynn at the table sharing a meal with me, and the out of control smoky fire in the fireplace. Well, most of my memories were good.

"Are you ready?" Brynn leaned against the Jeep as though she didn't have a care in the world, but I could sense her tension ten feet away. She was wound tight. If things between us were different, I would've suggested a quick remedy for relieving her stress. I was stressed, too, but I felt safe because of her. It wasn't fair. She gave me relief and I gave her high blood pressure.

"I can get a different car and find a different place. I didn't call you because I wanted you to come to my rescue again." That was a lie. "I called because I have photos of poachers and as soon as I can get connected to a workstation, I can download the photos and email them to you. I just didn't know what law enforcement agency to call, but I'm guessing you do." Why was I sabotaging this? Wasn't this what I wanted? Brynn Coleman in close proximity to me twenty-four hours a day?

She rubbed her face with her palms a few times and massaged the back of her neck for a few seconds before answering me. "I would feel better if you stayed with me. I don't think you realize the position you're in. We don't know who these guys are yet. I would just feel better if you were close by."

"Brynn, you don't have time to spare. I'm here for two more weeks and I can't take you from your job. That's not fair of me," I said.

"If they found you and hurt you, I'd never be able to live with myself," she said. "I feel responsible for you."

"Well, you aren't. I know you don't believe me and I can't even believe I'm saying this, but I'm an adult. Even though I've sucked out here in the wilderness, I'm pretty responsible in my real life. I thought I handled the situation with those hunters well." I left out the part where I shook the entire drive back and cried when Cee first saw my face. I was tired of Brynn seeing me cry.

She walked over to me and stood imposingly in my space. I didn't move. She looked at me. "I know things are awkward between us, but don't let your pride get in the way. I don't want you to get hurt. Just stay with me for a few days until we get this under control. Can you do that?" she asked. I sighed and wondered if she was right about pride. "Give me a few days to work with law enforcement. I know a state trooper who would love to help out. I'll see that she puts this top of her list. She owes me."

That answered the question of who I was supposed to call. I was going to say so, but instead I said, "A woman state trooper?" I couldn't have sounded more sexist, but Alaska didn't strike me as a forward thinking state.

"You sound surprised. Yes, she's been one for about a dozen or so years now. She's well respected. Once we get you settled,

I'll give her a call. We should probably get out of here. Follow me back to the airport."

I climbed into my car and wished I didn't have to drive back into town. I wanted to already be at Brynn's cabin, under a warm blanket, sitting by a properly contained fire. Brynn drove the speed limit the entire way. I wanted to get there fast, but patiently followed her instead. She was sacrificing her time to help me out. When we pulled up to the rental place, I swore they all pointed to me. I was infamous here. For the first time in an hour, I saw Brynn smile.

"They looked scared." She leaned in my window and watched me clean out the console.

I had an M&M problem based on the three crumpled empty wrappers smooshed in one of the cup holders. Diet definitely gone. When I turned to look at her, I gasped. She was very close to my face. She looked at my lips, then met my gaze and took a step back from the window.

"Ready?" She didn't give me a chance to answer, but opened my door and waited for me to climb out.

"Just doing a last minute sweep." I opened up the back doors and checked under the seats. Since I packed in a panic, I wasn't sure I had everything. Brynn lifted the hatch and poked around the back.

"All clear here," she said.

I locked the car and went inside to return it. The clerk gulped when I approached the counter. "I just need to turn the car in." I placed the keys on the counter.

"She's going home. She's had enough of this Alaskan wilderness. It's not for everyone." Brynn nudged my leg when she saw I was getting ready to say something to defend myself.

"Uh, yeah. I miss my life in the lower forty-eight." I heard somebody say that at the diner the other day.

"Sure. Just give me a few minutes to check you out. You can have a seat if you want." They had to inspect the SUV and I couldn't blame them.

Brynn stretched her arm out and rested it on the back of my chair. It felt like such a possessive move. I wanted to lean back into her. Had anybody else done that, I would've asked them to move it.

"You can borrow my truck or the sedan I've been working on." Her voice was low enough for only me to hear. She held her hand up when I started protesting. "Just for a few days. Until we get a better handle on what's going on. Besides, you'll be my shadow for at least the next three or four days so you won't even need a car."

I sighed. This wasn't the place to have this conversation. I jumped up when the clerk motioned me forward to the counter.

"You're all set. Please just sign here and here, and you're good to go." He pointed to three blanks and I happily signed. I took my receipt and bolted out the door that Brynn held open. I climbed into the passenger side of Brynn's car and watched Brynn gracefully slide into the driver's seat. She had the longest legs I'd seen on a woman who wasn't a model. The memory of our legs entwined on her bed flashed in my mind. I'd wanted her to strip me down and make me hers that day. I inhaled sharply at the intensity of it, drawing unnecessary attention to myself.

"I know you aren't happy about this, but I'm just looking out for you," she said.

Thankfully, she didn't know where my thoughts were. "I know. And thank you for looking out for me. I'm not trying to be difficult. This is all just so new to me and I'm glad I have you on my side to help me out."

Brynn's expression became serious. We spent the rest of the drive in silence. The realization of what happened and what could have happened finally set in. I couldn't stop shaking.

Brynn reached over and rubbed my arm until we reached her cabin. "Come on. Let's get you inside and comfortable. I'll get your luggage in a few minutes," she said. I didn't argue. I slid out of the Jeep and followed her inside. She grabbed a blanket and pointed to an oversized chair near the fireplace. "Here. Have a seat." I sat and she gently tucked the blanket around me. "I'm going to get your things from the Jeep so just sit back and relax." I nodded and watched her through the screen door as she grabbed all three bags and my jacket and made her way back inside. She put my things in her bedroom and shut the door on her way out. "I'll be sleeping in the other room. I remembered you liked my bedroom a lot." She avoided eye contact. I watched her slip off her jacket. Her uniform was still neatly pressed against her, but there was a small line of sweat on her back. She loosened her tie, unbuttoned the top button and rolled up her sleeves. She was so damn sexy doing simple everyday things. "Are you cold? Do you want a cup of tea?"

"Tea would be great." I grew tired when the adrenaline left my body. The only thing I could think about was closing my eyes. Maybe I dreamed it, but I thought I felt Brynn's fingers brush the hair away from my cheek and touch my face. When I woke up, she was gone, but there was a cup of tea on the table closest to me, the water lukewarm. There was a note by the cup and for the first time all afternoon, I smiled.

I had to go the sanctuary to finish a few things there. The cabin's locked up. I should be back soon. Oh, and I'm bringing a friend. I hope that's okay.

I smiled at the really bad drawing of Wally and tucked the note into my jeans. I couldn't wait to see both of them again.

CHAPTER FIFTEEN

I was in Brynn's room when I heard her unlock the front door. I walked back into the living room with my laptop and camera. Wally was standing on his hind legs, sniffing. When he saw me he walked over and reached up. I put the camera on the couch and bent to scratch behind his ears and under his chin.

"Hello, big boy. How was your day?" He chirped his response and waddled back to Brynn. I looked at her and smiled. "Thanks for leaving me the note. I'm sorry I fell asleep."

She held up her hands and waved me off. "Completely understandable given the circumstances. Do you feel better?"

I nodded. "I do. Thank you for letting me nap."

"Are you hungry? I could make dinner if you want." She opened the refrigerator and poked around. "I can throw some steaks out on the grill, or some fish. Or we can go all out and eat cheesy pasta or pizza. Anything you want."

"I'm starving," I said.

"You could have helped yourself to anything in my place, you know. I think I might even have some M&Ms."

I blushed. She saw my not-so-hidden chocolate stash in my rental. "Oh, I wouldn't pry. I knew you would be back soon." That sounded breathier than I intended. Or maybe I meant it. I looked away.

"Well, just know nothing's off limits. Okay?"

"Thank you. For everything." I found it hard to look at her because even though she offered everything, she herself was off-limits. It was the one thing I wanted in this house. I had to settle for food. For now. "And a steak actually sounds good. As much as I've enjoyed all of the different fishes and meats, I just miss a good old-fashioned steak. Medium. Salt and pepper." Not that she asked how to prepare mine.

"Great. How about a baked potato, too?"

I nodded. I realized that I had a cup of coffee today and a cookie that Cee made me eat. That was it. No wonder I had the shakes. I needed protein. I stood up. "Let me help."

"Absolutely not. I want you to relax. Keep Wally company. I'll have dinner ready in no time."

I sat and watched Brynn work. She was quick, and quiet, and I didn't want to interrupt her. She sliced cheddar cheese, a crisp apple, and handed me a plate. I was so happy to have food.

"Can I give Wally any of this?" Wally was on the other end of the couch watching me. I could tell she wasn't happy with the idea, but she couldn't tell me no. At least not about this.

"Okay. You can give him an apple slice, but that's it. I don't want to spoil his dinner," she said.

Once I had food in my stomach, I wanted do something except sit and wait for Brynn to serve dinner. I opened up my laptop and downloaded the incriminating photos of the poachers. Even though they were taken from far away, I found several where the men's faces were clear and recognizable. I also transferred the photos from my phone to the laptop. They were lower quality, but I included them in the file anyway. I dug inside of my bag until I found a flash drive. I uploaded the pictures and had it ready for Brynn right when dinner was ready. Great timing.

"I asked Lara Ridgley, that state trooper, to come over tonight after her shift. I hope you are comfortable talking to her." Brynn sat in front of her plate.

"That's fine." I had freshened up after my nap, but I was still in need of a shower. I was sure all of the leaves were gone from my hair, but I didn't feel clean. "I have all the photos saved to the flash drive. Maybe her department can read the fuzzy license plates. The camera on my phone wasn't on the highest quality setting." I dug into my steak and moaned. "Brynn, this dinner's fantastic. It's exactly what I needed." I stopped talking until I cleaned my plate.

Brynn smiled at me the entire dinner. After taking care of Wally, she asked to look through the photos before Lara stopped by. We grabbed our drinks and sat on the couch with plenty of room between us. I had to move the laptop over just so she could see them better. She concentrated hard on the photos and I took the time to study her. It was hard not to stare at her generous mouth, or the way her lips parted slightly as she concentrated on studying the photos. They were so red, and only marred by the tiny scar that nicked the corner of her bottom lip. I wanted to kiss it because it was perfectly imperfect. When she turned to face me, I realized I was too close and slowly leaned back. We heard a car pull up.

"I don't know these guys, but hopefully Lara does." Brynn's shoulders relaxed when she looked out of the window. "She's here."

I stood for no other reason than I felt like I was in trouble. Law enforcement made me nervous. I'd never broken any law except for parking in the wrong spot. I smiled when I saw the trooper. She was a beautiful woman with long brown hair and a nice smile. She walked to me and reached out to shake my hand.

"So nice to meet you, Kennedy. I'm sorry you had such a horrible experience today, but I'm glad you made it out okay. We're going to do everything we can to catch these guys." She took off her brown jacket and hung it on the back of a chair. She was comfortable here. There weren't any rings on her fingers, or any jewelry on her at all. "I missed dinner?" She smiled at Brynn who shrugged at her.

"I invited you but you were too busy having dinner with the mayor or the governor or somebody like that," Brynn said. She winked at Lara. Winked at her! They were too familiar with one another. I bet they dated.

"I just couldn't get out of it. You know what these things are like," Lara said.

"That I do." They smiled at one another again. "If you're hungry, I can fix you something."

"So, I have a flash drive with all of the photos that you can take back to the station with you." I was a jerk for interrupting their memories, but I was tired of watching them flirt back and forth.

"Oh, yes. So let's talk about where you were and what happened." Lara sat next to me on the couch and scrolled through the photos. I told her everything I could remember from what they were wearing, to the tattoos on their arms and necks. She asked about their accents and mannerisms, things that couldn't be determined from pictures alone. She was thorough and smart. I learned a few interviewing tips from her.

"Do you catch a lot of poachers?" I asked.

"Unfortunately, a lot of them get away, so whenever we do catch them, we're careful and ensure we do everything by the book. Thank you for these photos. You were brave to do this and come forward. I'm glad you got away before anything happened." She put her hand on my forearm in a reassuring way.

"I was stupid for going out there alone in the first place," I said.

"No, you weren't. For the most part, this area's relatively secure," she said.

"Yeah, but this area has never met Kennedy Wells," Brynn said.

I shot her a mean look. It was hard to keep it because she was smiling at me. A small dimple high on her left cheek appeared that I hadn't noticed before. I decided not to fight the truth. I turned to Lara. "She's right. I've had nothing but bad luck since I landed. Not even kidding."

"Oh, are you the one who had the encounter with the moose?" she asked.

"Does everybody know?"

Brynn busted out laughing. "I told you it was a good story to tell at our potluck dinner."

"I didn't think you were serious," I said.

"Kennedy, don't worry. I know it was an awful thing to experience, but it was tame compared to a lot of things we see and hear here. Don't let Brynn get under your skin like that. She's just teasing." Lara shot a grin at Brynn. "Maybe we should talk about what happened when she first got here." Lara dropped that bomb and both Brynn and I pounced at the same time.

"Don't you dare—" Brynn scrambled into the living room.

"Tell me everything." I planted myself between Brynn and Lara. I shuddered when I felt Brynn's hands playfully pull my elbows back until my back was pressed against her body. Her laughter in my ear made me shudder. She was too close and my body betrayed me.

"Let's keep in mind that I was twenty years old. I didn't know any better," Brynn said.

"Are you kidding me? Like I've known any better? Oh, please do tell, Lara."

Brynn groaned and threw herself on the couch in pretend agony. "Go ahead. Destroy my cool factor."

Lara rubbed her hand over Brynn's short hair. "So we get this call about somebody stuck in a Porta Potti at one of the trailheads. My partner and I were a few miles away. We got to the site and see this Porta Potti on its side completely ripped to shreds," Lara said.

Brynn groaned again and hid her face under a pillow, interrupting the story.

"Oh, don't stop. This is too good." I leaned forward to encourage Lara.

"Well, the call came from inside the Porta Potti. Apparently this new, wet behind the ears ranger got chased by a bear and that was the only place she could get to safety. Never mind that her truck was twenty feet away and definitely safer than a plastic box. The bear tipped over the Porta Potti and tried to rip into it. Eventually, it left. By the time we got there, a sweet, albeit angry, Brynn was covered in crap and angrier than I had ever seen anybody before." Lara paused to laugh at the memory while Brynn continued to groan. "We had to pry off the top to get her out. It beat rolling it over again because when the bear tipped it, it fell on the door side. Brynn wasn't happy with the idea of rolling it one more time."

"I wish I could have seen it." I laughed at the image of Brynn covered in waste and super pissed off.

"Oh, it gets better. She crawls out and yells every profanity I've ever heard while stripping down to nothing. She didn't care that we didn't know her or that my partner was a guy. She took everything off and marched over to her truck and washed off with several bottles of water and an old T-shirt."

Brynn dramatically punched the pillow that covered her face. "It was the worst thing ever. I took a million showers with strong soap. It took forever to get the smell off. To this day, I refuse to go in any kind of outhouse," she said.

"After she cleaned up the best she could, she came back over to us and introduced herself wearing a tank, a pair of boxers, and waders. She was so unbelievably cute," Lara said.

Another shared look between them. I was starting to feel like a third wheel. "Suddenly my moose story isn't that bad," I said. Brynn's story won, hands down.

"Not at all. And that's just the beginning," Lara said.

"Okay, okay. We're done here. Let's focus on Kennedy and a game plan," Brynn said. That sobered us up.

Lara slipped back into professional mode and told us what her department was going to concentrate on and what I should do. She also recommended that I stay with Brynn because nobody knew I was there.

"And I want in on this, Lara. I want you to keep me posted and if you need more people out looking, I can recruit some of the rangers. They hate poachers too," Brynn said.

"Here's my business card. If you remember anything else, please text me or call me, day or night. Okay?" Lara smiled at me and handed me her card. Out of the corner of my eye, I saw Brynn frown and I didn't know if it was because Lara gave me her card, or that I accepted it with a smile on my face.

CHAPTER SIXTEEN

I'm going to try to send out other rangers for the calls that come in." Brynn turned her truck into the sanctuary's parking lot. Wally stood up between us when we slowed down.

"Oh, I don't mind going with you. Please, don't let this whole thing get in the way of you doing your job. Plus, I can call it research. I can work from anywhere." I pointed to my messenger bag. "On-the-go-office. I'm used to it."

"Don't worry about it. Truly. We help one another out all of the time. Everybody's aware of the situation. We'll find these guys. I promise. We'll still go out on some rescues, but just the small ones. Like Owlie," Brynn said.

"Oh, I missed his release. How did he do?" All because I couldn't handle the fact that Brynn rejected me. That would've been a great photo.

"He did well. He hopped around and at first I wasn't sure he was going to fly, but eventually he stretched out his wings and took off. It was beautiful," she said.

"I'm sorry I missed it."

Brynn nodded. "So let me drop Wally off and we'll grab the Jeep and start making our rounds. If you want, we can even swing by the wharf if you need to interview anybody."

"Let's make today about the sanctuary. I have more than enough information and interviews to write my fishing article. I'm in it for photos at this point," I said.

I petted Wally good-bye and waited at the Jeep for Brynn. When she returned, she walked down the ramp toward me, confident and strong. I watched her the entire time. She knew I wanted her. She knew the effect she had on me. I decided not to hide it anymore. The decision was hers. Either she would act on it or not.

"Ready?" She stopped in front of me.

I wanted to reach out and straighten her tie, but I refrained. "I'm ready."

The morning was spent hitting all of the trailheads near the sanctuary. Brynn was keeping an eye out for the two trucks with distinctive trailers. I couldn't imagine they would show up knowing there was an eyewitness out there. I know if I did something illegal and somebody saw my face, I would be long gone.

Lunch break was in town, surrounded by a lot of people. I'm sure Brynn did that so that we wouldn't have a repeat of our last attempt at lunch. The one where I rubbed against her and I felt her kiss all the way to my core. Our conversation was light and was more about our jobs.

"Do you see yourself working for the magazine for the rest of your life?" Brynn asked.

That was a difficult question. I wanted to, but I also hated the idea of that being my only identity. Being away from the limelight, I was so used to made me think about my decisions. Did I want the kind of relationship Mandy and Lisa had? Was I even capable of that kind of love? Watching them stirred feelings inside of me and reminded me there was more to a relationship than sex. There was trust, communication, loyalty, all of which I had little to no experience with even though I was thirty-one.

"Yes and no. It would be hard to have the career I have and settle down with somebody. I would have to sacrifice, and let's face it, I'm not the kind of girl who likes to sacrifice." Even as I said those words, I doubted them. I had it in me to love somebody unconditionally, but I was afraid it was buried so deeply that I wouldn't ever find it. "What about you? Is Alaska forever? Would you ever want to move back to Florida or somewhere else?"

Brynn slowly twirled the almost empty coffee cup in her hands. "I've been here a long time, but I like it. It has the small town life, the love thy neighbor mentality. And I love my job here. I love animals. I was going to school to become a veterinarian at Florida State."

"Did you think about going to school here for that? The university probably has a good program given that ratio of wild animals to people is a million to one," I said.

Brynn laughed. "It's not that bad. Besides, I have a lot of hands-on experience. Tina's a great teacher. She's patient with me. I help her out whenever I can. Most of my job is out in the field, though, where I'm fumbling along," she said.

"You never fumble. You're so good with animals and you seem so sure about everything you do," I said.

"Not everything, but thank you. I've toyed with the idea of going back to school. Not that any of my credits would transfer. I'd have to start over." She grabbed the bill before I even saw the waitress drop it on the table.

"I have an expense account. You should at least let me buy you lunch since you are carting me around everywhere," I said.

She shook her head at me. "Nope. My idea, my treat."

I wanted to ask so many questions, but I didn't want her to know that I had been snooping on the internet and found out more about her than she had admitted to me. Maybe she would never tell me. The reporter in me hated that, but the woman in me understood. Not everybody wanted their dirty laundry out there, especially me.

"Do you want me to start a fire?"

I looked up from my laptop and stared at Brynn. I was completely engrossed in writing. I wasn't working on the fishing story, but a journal where I started writing my thoughts and experiences in Alaska because I didn't want to forget anything that happened. It was different for me and even though I wasn't a great communicator in person, I could write my raw, unedited emotions well. It took a few seconds to process what she asked.

"Sure, if you don't mind." I looked at the clock and couldn't believe it was already nine.

Wally was playing with an empty paper towel roll in the kitchen. I could watch him for hours, but I knew that I had to stay focused. My time was limited. Both of my stories were progressing, but I wanted to take a step away from them. Brynn had been unusually quiet at dinner. I figured she had things on her mind, so I mentally checked out. For two hours, I had been writing a journal of my time spent here from my first harrowing hours until right before Brynn's lips touched mine the first time. I was at a good stopping point.

"Would you like a cup of tea?" I asked. After arguing like an old married couple at the grocery store earlier this evening, Brynn agreed to let me buy the first round of groceries.

"That sounds great," she said.

I put the kettle on the stove and watched her build a fire. She made making a fire seem like an art form. The placement of the logs and the kindling was perfectly symmetrical, so very different than mine. I decided right then that I would never attempt a fire again unless it was the apocalypse and I was the only one left. Who was I kidding? I'd probably be one of the first to die. Alaska picked me up by the scruff, shook me, and showed me I was no match for her. I was a city girl through and through.

"What are you smiling about?" Brynn asked.

I laughed because my thoughts were ridiculous and she probably wouldn't understand my sense of humor. "I was just thinking about the one and only time I built a fire." I was rewarded with a smug smile. "I know, I know. I will never even think about that here. Your cabin's immaculate. Are you sure you want this tornado of a woman in your place?"

"Are you kidding me? I live with a raccoon. You've got nothing on him," she said.

The night before, Brynn made me shut my door and gave me earplugs. I told her I didn't need them, but she told me to take them anyway. I quickly learned the real reason Brynn's cabin was spotless with little décor. Raccoons were nocturnal and Wally liked to play hockey in the middle of the night with things that weren't nailed down. I couldn't get the plugs deep enough in my ears. He kept slipping his little paw under the door, jiggling it just enough to make a soft bumping noise. I finally opened it. He sniffed around the room and climbed over me several times which freaked me out so I turned on the lamp by the bed. Raccoons in the day were cute. Raccoons at night? A little scary. Thankfully, my luggage and personal items were stored in the closet out of his reach. Eventually, he grew tired of me and left the room. I fell asleep with the light on.

"You've never seen me when I'm sleep deprived. Or close to a deadline," I said.

"Aren't you close to a deadline now?" She poked the fire and brushed her hands on her jeans. Even dressed casually, she looked great. I was in pajama bottoms and a sweatshirt. If she wasn't interested in me, I wasn't going to waste my energy trying anymore. My long hair was piled high on my head, and because my eyes were tired, I was wearing my glasses. Not the cool librarian ones, but the nerdy I need to see everything in my peripheral vision ones that almost magnified my face. I was the exact opposite of sexy right now.

"I have time. Both stories are practically done." I sat up a little higher when she sat on the couch, her knee brushing mine. She put her hand on my knee apologetically and I shivered at her touch. "I've been thinking." I wanted to ease into this idea so I took it slow and gave her a nice smile.

"Okay." She dragged the word out. She furrowed her brow. I wanted to smooth it out with a touch or a kiss, but stopped short of reaching out to her.

"How about if I stay here at the cabin tomorrow when you go to work. I'll keep to myself. I will stay right here on this couch." I patted the couch.

"No."

"What do you mean 'no'? Brynn, nobody knows I'm here. Nobody knows that we're friends. Chances are, those hunters are long gone," I said. She looked like she was considering it. I pushed harder. "I promise to stay inside. Right here."

"I don't know, Kennedy. I would feel better if you were with me." She rubbed her hands nervously on her jeans.

"Come on. This is the safest place on Earth. You see how easy it is to get lost when I write. I don't even remember the last two hours. I would get so much done."

"Well, if you need the time, I guess it makes sense." She seemed to relax after coming to that decision. "You're right. Nobody knows where you are. Just don't get upset if I call you several times."

"Did Lara have any information?" Lara called Brynn while we were at lunch. Brynn missed the call and didn't realize it for several hours.

Brynn sighed heavily. "No, they weren't able to enhance the photo, unfortunately. Lara said they are reasonably certain they are Alaskan license plates, but they couldn't even confirm that. Her department is tracking down all makes and models of both trucks. It's just going to take some time." All of the plates had been mud spattered. I wondered if that was strategic to make them difficult to identify.

"I think it's sweet that you have taken on the role of my protector, but I don't think all of this is necessary. You've gone above and beyond for me."

"We're friends. I take care of my friends," she said.

"So." I started because it was the perfect segue and I couldn't help myself. "Speaking of friends, tell me about you and Lara. You seem pretty close and comfortable with one another." Did I just sound jealous? "Is there a story there?"

"Always the reporter, huh?" She laughed.

She stood and went into the kitchen to pour more hot water in her cup. She looked out the kitchen window for a few moments. I waited patiently even though my curiosity was tearing me up inside. I felt queasy.

"We tried dating when I was real young. Right after the Porta Potti incident. We went out a few times, but decided it would be best to be friends," she said.

"That's it? That's all I get?" I wanted every juicy detail. Not really. Just more than what she gave me.

"There's nothing else to tell. We were at different points in our lives. I was just getting started. A baby dyke who wasn't even old enough to drink. She was older and wanted a relationship. I didn't. I wasn't over my girlfriend in Florida." She sat back on the couch, this time closer to me.

"What about now? Is she taken?"

"No."

"No? That's it? Nothing else?" I was dying to know why they weren't trying. "You obviously have your shit together now."

"I have a lot of respect for Lara, but that's it. We will only ever be strictly platonic." Her explanation was vague and boring. Something happened, but she wasn't going to tell me. I got the sense the real story had nothing to do with Lara. Brynn was driving me crazy with her secrecy. I had no right, but I wanted to get to know her better.

I had no response. We sat and stared at the fire until we were both uncomfortable. Brynn shifted her weight, crossed and uncrossed her arms, and eventually stood to stoke the fire. The room was getting smaller and smaller by the minute. I decided to make my retreat.

"Okay, well, I'm going to bed. Thanks again for cooking dinner and letting me write," I said.

"It wasn't a problem. I was cooking anyway."

I bristled at her explanation. She was pulling away from me and I wasn't sure why.

"Thanks. I'll see you tomorrow. If I'm not up when you leave, have a good day." I headed to the bedroom and shut the door, sad that our evening ended with a fizzle. I didn't even get to say good night to Wally.

CHAPTER SEVENTEEN

It was noon, and I was tired of being cooped up inside. I finished writing for the morning and decided to have a cup of tea out on the porch. The sun was shining after an early morning downpour. The afternoon was supposed to be on the warmish side. I threw on jeans, a T-shirt, and one of Brynn's quilted flannel shirts that was hanging on the back of a kitchen chair. It was large on me, but it smelled like her. I was sure she wouldn't mind. Our few days together in her cabin were nice and amicable, but I still wanted her. Every so often, I would get a rush of heat when I caught her staring at me. She would smile nervously and look away. She was so hard to read. I poured my tea and headed outside with a rival magazine of *A&A*. It was always a good idea to keep up with the competition and I liked mindlessly thumbing through tangible pages instead of reading on my laptop. My eyes needed a break from the computer screen.

I loved that Brynn had large wooden rocking chairs on her porch. Flower boxes draped over the railings held fresh soil. Brynn must have recently planted bulbs or seeds. A red and white bird feeder hung from the corner that faced east and a butterfly house stood tall several feet from the porch. The country look wasn't something I would have gone for, but it added to the charm of the place.

It was too quiet though. I heard birds, but no traffic, no people, no hustle of city living. I needed music. I headed back inside to grab my phone, but I couldn't get back into the cabin. I jiggled the handle several times, the first time in disbelief and the ten after that in total panic. The door wasn't going to open no matter how hard I pushed, pulled, or threw myself against it. I was locked out. I leaned my head against the door and sighed. Of course. My awesome luck continued. I tried all of the windows and the back door, but nothing budged.

My heart sank. Not because I was scared, but that my phone—my contact to the outside world—was inside. I couldn't believe I left it behind. I usually had it within reach at all times. Alaska was making me too soft and comfortable.

The good news was that bad people and enraged animals weren't chasing me. I was safe, yet alone here. Brynn's closest neighbor was a few miles away. I had several hours to kill until Brynn showed up, so instead of freaking out, I took a deep breath and forced myself to relax. I decided to wander around Brynn's property. I grabbed a walking stick I found next to the stairs to use as a means of protection and headed out past the shed to the great unknown. At least I had a decent breakfast so my energy level was high. The wind picked up when I climbed to the top of the hill. I buttoned Brynn's shirt and snuggled in its warmth. Who knew someone could look so sexy in such practical clothes?

The view where I stood was spectacular. I was bummed that I didn't have my camera though. Brynn should've built her house up here. Mountains in every direction, budding wildflowers, and fresh air. For some reason, I felt safe. Maybe it was because I was wearing Brynn's shirt or that I was standing in her little piece of the world, but I feared nothing. I had never known peace like this. I finally understood why Brynn stayed in Alaska. I just wanted to know the whole story of why she was here in the first place. I put my life in the hands of a stranger. What did I really know about her?

"Kennedy." I heard the panic in Brynn's voice before I saw it on her face. She marched up the hill toward me. Her eyes were almost black by the time she reached me. I reached out to touch her arms. Her body was tense under my fingertips.

"I'm so sorry. I locked myself out of your house. I went to have tea on the porch and forgot to unlock the door. I also left my phone on the kitchen counter. I'm fine though."

"I was so worried. You didn't answer my texts or calls and I feared the worse." She took off her jacket and put it around my shoulders. I wasn't cold, but I didn't want to be rude so I thanked her.

"I'm fine. I couldn't break into your house, which is good news, but I got bored and decided to go for a walk. This is such a beautiful place, Brynn."

"Listen, Kennedy. I heard from Cee and Lara." She took a deep breath and rubbed her hands over her face, a gesture I'd come to know as her way of calming down. "Cee said a guy asked about you yesterday. Then, last night, the cabin you were staying in was ransacked. She and John contacted the police. They spent the morning with Lara looking through photos at the station. The guy who asked about you wasn't one of the three you had a run-in with." She waited for the news to sink in.

I stared at her for at least ten seconds while I processed the information, but I couldn't understand. "So what does that mean?"

"Apparently this is bigger than we thought. Showing up at the cabins was a dumb move, but vandalizing one of them is a lot more serious. These guys mean business."

"What the hell did I stumble on?" I wanted to lean on Brynn for support, but the look in her eyes told me now wasn't the time to do it.

"Lara's getting the Alaska Department of Fish and Game involved, which means more resources for the investigation. Cee didn't have a way to get a photo of the guy who visited her, but she gave a detailed description. With your photos and the incidents at Cee's cabins, we have enough to get outside help. The locals can only do so much so I feel better about that," she said. I didn't know Brynn that well, but I'd never seen her so visibly worried. She was upset the other day when she insisted I say at her cabin, but not to this extent.

"Well, I don't think I'll be here much longer. I'm sure my boss doesn't need the publicity of one of her writers getting caught up in a poaching ring." I almost smiled knowing Erin was going to completely lose her shit at my latest saga. I hadn't told her yet because I honestly just thought it was a couple of dumbasses making bad decisions. I figured they'd be slapped with a large fine and be on their way.

"You aren't caught up. You're a witness. There's a difference," Brynn said. "Are you ready to get warm by the fire? I'm sure my shirt isn't exactly warm." Busted.

"I didn't want to wear a coat because the sun felt good and your shirt was within reach. I hope you don't mind that I wore it." I wasn't going to admit that it smelled like her and wearing it made me feel closer to her.

"No, it's fine. I'm just happy you had something somewhat warm. When the sun disappears, it gets cold. Spring isn't the same here as it is in California." We headed back to her house where she showed me a secret hiding place in the railing where there was a key.

"Now you can get into my house any time you want." She pointed at the smaller shed. "And that has a code you can punch and get inside. It's not heated, but at least it will get you out of the elements. I have a portable stove in there, too."

"This won't happen again. I'm not going to leave without checking the door a thousand times first. Plus, I can get in the front door, thanks to the secret key," I said.

Brynn quickly unlocked the front door and ushered me inside. "I'll start a fire."

I liked watching Brynn work. She was lean and sinewy, and I enjoyed seeing her muscles bunch up under her uniform as she stacked the logs and quickly lit them. I wondered if her uniform was comfortable. It fit her like a glove, but didn't seem to restrict her. It had to have been specifically tailored to fit. Nobody got that lucky off of the rack.

"Do you mind if I take a shower? I think that will warm me the quickest. I won't be long."

She nodded and continued working on the fireplace. "I'll have a cup of tea ready for you when you return." Her smile was sweet, but it didn't reach her eyes. She was worried about me.

I didn't know how to feel about any of it. The fact that people were looking for me felt surreal. Until this point, my life had been straightforward. I focused on work and climbed that ladder. I never got into trouble, had only a few parking tickets on my record, and paid my bills on time. Sure, I was in the public eye, but never for anything bad. No death threats, nobody chased me, no real drama except that one, teeny, tiny indiscretion. That felt huge at the time, but nothing like this.

Brynn was taking charge of me and I was allowing it. I didn't mind that somebody was watching over me. I felt like I mattered for the first time in a long time. I was changing. I hopped out of the shower and put on my pajamas pants, a sweatshirt, and thick socks. My wardrobe was lacking, but I didn't care. I was in a cabin being guarded by a strong, beautiful dyke.

"You can borrow a pair of sweats. I can't imagine those keep you warm." Brynn pointed to a cup of steaming tea on the coffee table in front of my seat. "And that's your cup of tea."

"Where's Wally?" I didn't remember seeing him when Brynn let us into the cabin.

"I left him at the sanctuary. Tonight he has a sleepover at Tina's," she said.

I frowned because I missed him. "Does he have a lot of sleepovers?"

"Normally, no, but I panicked when I couldn't reach you so she volunteered to watch him while I figured out what happened to you." She sat in the chair to my left and stretched her long legs under the table. She had changed into an Alaskan Wildlife Rescue sweatshirt and a pair of jeans. I missed the uniform.

"Remind me to buy a sweatshirt tomorrow at the sanctuary. I like the look of it," I said. The navy color made Brynn's eyes stand out.

"I'd give you this one, but you are so tiny, I'd have to wrap it around you twice to get it to fit."

"I did wear your shirt today," I said.

"Yes, and you looked like a waif." For some reason, that hurt my feelings. She must have sensed that it upset me. "I mean, I'm huge compared to you. We could never share clothes. I would tear yours up if I tried on your pajamas or your sweaters." That didn't make me feel any better. I nodded and turned my attention back to the fire. All of this was so strange to me. My fate was in the hands of somebody I didn't know. I trusted Brynn, but I felt vulnerable. I was out of my element and I didn't know how to handle my emotions.

"Okay, well, I guess I'm going to go to bed early." I stood. Brynn jumped up next to me.

"It's not even seven yet. Aren't you hungry? Do you want me to make some dinner?" she asked. Her hand rested on my forearm. She didn't want me to leave, but for some reason, I had to.

"I probably just need to lie down. I'll pass on dinner. I got to keep this waifish figure." I didn't know why I was being snarky. She moved her hand away from me and walked into the kitchen. I rolled my eyes at myself. I could be such an ass. "Thanks for rescuing me. Again." I headed to my room and closed the door as quietly as I could. I was trapped. Sleep didn't sound like such a bad idea. I pulled back the covers and slipped into bed. My mood was dark and I needed time to process my feelings. I was starting to care and I didn't like how vulnerable that made me.

CHAPTER EIGHTEEN

I was disoriented when I woke up. For a split second, I forgot where I was. It was dark and quiet. Wally wasn't in the cabin wrestling with something. I remembered he was at a slumber party at Tina's. It was hot so I threw off the covers and kicked them off of the bed. I was drowsy, but not enough to fall back to sleep. I padded over to the bathroom and drank a glass of cold water. I stripped to my panties and my tank top hoping to cool off. Why was it so hot in this room?

I opened the door softly and walked to the kitchen. The water made my stomach gurgle, reminding me I was hungry. I opened the refrigerator, pulled out a peach, and stood over the kitchen sink to eat it. I peered out the window and watched the night. Alaska noises at midnight were different than L.A. noises. I would fail any basic animal sound identification test. It was so creepy that I actually lowered my head at one point as if the animals could see me staring out. I saw movement behind some trees, but I didn't know if it was a fox, or a wolf, or the shadow of a tree moving in the night's sudden breeze. There was no way I could live here in the middle of nowhere with noises like that.

"What do you see?" Brynn unintentionally sneaked up behind me to look out the window, too.

I didn't hear her approach so I screamed. "What the fuck, Brynn? You just can't come out of nowhere like that." I was breathing hard and pissed that she scared me.

The corner of her mouth held the beginning of a smile and she was trying not to laugh. She put her hands on either side of me, her fingers curled around the edge of the sink. "I'm sorry. I thought you heard me." She looked me in the eye, then I watched as her gaze traveled the length of my body to see what little I was wearing. I felt my nipples harden under her gaze. "Are you cold?" I shifted my weight from one foot to the other. She was in my personal space and wasn't backing off. I felt a drop of peach juice on my cheek and wiped it off with the back of my hand. "No. I was actually hot and hungry and decided to come out for a snack. I found the peaches." She was still close to me. I could feel her body heat and I shivered.

"Do you always shiver when you're hot?" She licked her lips. This was a very different and very confident Brynn standing in front of me, only inches from my body.

I looked up at her and challenged her. "Only when I can feel somebody I want close to me." She already knew I wanted her, so why not keep baiting her? She moved closer to me. I could feel her bare leg touching the outside of mine. I had to look up to meet her eyes. My heart leapt as she lowered her head and nuzzled her lips against mine.

"Do you want me close to you?"

My only answer was a slight moan. I opened my mouth as she ran her tongue gently over my bottom lip. As much as I wanted to press myself against her, I needed to know she wasn't going to start something and not finish again. "Are you going to run away again?" This ache, this need, was too strong. I couldn't handle rejection a third time.

She answered me by tilting my head away and kissing my neck. Her hands gripped my hips and slid down to my ass as her mouth found mine. She lifted me up so I was sitting on the edge of the sink and pulled my legs to wrap around her waist. I guess that answered my question. She slipped her hands under my tank and tugged it over my head. I forgot about the sounds outside. I only heard the rush of my heartbeat and the hitch in her breath.

"Do you want me to stop?" She was waiting for permission. My legs were wrapped around her and I was almost completely naked. Short of flashing a neon sign that spelled "yes," my answer was loud and clear.

"Don't even think about it." I felt a small smile on her lips before she kissed me deeply. I moaned when I felt her fingers slide under the silky material of my panties and pull them down. I had to shift my weight from side to side until they were at my knees.

Brynn stepped away from between my legs to yank them completely off. She carried me to the couch. I was desperate for the feel of her on top of me. She placed a path of tender kisses down my body. I didn't want sweet. I wanted passion and heat. We had time later to go slow and be new lovers.

"Brynn, please don't make me wait any longer. I need you right now." I was breathless and desperate.

She wasted no time stripping off her T-shirt and boxer briefs. I hissed when she crawled between my legs and our bodies touched. I automatically wrapped my legs around her again. She pressed into me and we both moaned at the contact.

"You're so wet," she said and moved her hips into mine.

I released my legs from around her waist to give her more room. Maneuvering on the couch was restrictive, but I was too turned on to care. I was going to have my first of many orgasms in about thirty seconds if she continued to grind into me. She slipped her hand between our bodies. Her fingers rubbed up and down my swollen slit until I begged her to fuck me. I didn't think she heard me, but then I felt two deliciously long fingers slide into my core. I arched my back off of the couch as the feeling of being completely taken by another woman overtook my body. It was incredible.

I threw one leg on the back of the couch and put my other foot on the floor so I could move into her. She leaned back on her knees and watched me thrust against her hand. Her other hand rubbed all over my body, brushing over my erect nipples and sliding over my thighs. When she lowered her head and kissed my stomach, I squirmed and put my hands on her shoulders. I wanted her mouth on me. I clenched and tried to stop the first orgasm from exploding. Her lips weren't even to my hips before it hit. I cried out in surprise and frustration at my lack of control. She filled me in a way I hadn't felt before. She continued thrusting and put her mouth on my clit. It was only a matter of seconds before I felt myself climbing for another, more powerful orgasm.

"Please don't stop." I squeezed her shoulders to keep her in place and moved my hips against her mouth, finding the perfect friction. We both moaned when we realized I was going to come again. My body felt flushed. I tensed and cried out for the second time.

Brynn slowed her movements and gently slipped out of me when I tugged her up. I wanted to hold her. I wanted to feel her weight on top of me again. She kissed my shoulder and my neck, then softly sucked my earlobe. I felt a jolt through my whole body. I ran my hands over her sweaty back, anxious to touch her all over.

"Can we go back into the bedroom? I need more space," Brynn said.

I couldn't form a complete sentence yet and only managed a nod. She reached out and pulled me up. The sensation of her naked body against mine gave me a surge of energy. I couldn't wait to touch her. I led the way to my room because it had the bigger bed. She ignored the covers piled at the foot of the bed and pulled me onto the mattress.

"Why did I wait so long?" she asked.

I didn't have time to answer before her lips captured mine in another heated kiss. She twisted our bodies so that I was underneath her again. My body wouldn't be able to handle another orgasm so soon. As good as her touch felt, as wet as I was for her, my body needed to relax for a few minutes. I gently pushed her back and straddled her waist. She ran her hands over my breasts and down to my thighs. Her appetite for me was voracious. She leaned up so that we were face to face. I moaned when her fingers found my slit again. I leaned forward so she could slip inside, even though I was sure I wouldn't be able to come again so soon.

"More." I wanted to feel as much of her as I could.

She moaned louder than I did when she slid a third finger inside. I clung to her shoulders and rocked against her hand, fearing that my motions would hurt her. That fear wasn't enough to make me stop, because I was selfish and had wanted Brynn to fuck me since the second I laid eyes on her. I wanted to touch her at the same time, but I couldn't concentrate on anything except for her inside me, consuming me. We found the perfect rhythm together and I let myself go with wild abandonment. She held on to me, but gave me the room to move, to climb, until I reached climax again. I collapsed against her, my body shaking with absolute exhaustion.

"Come here, lie with me." She grabbed the sheets off the floor. I couldn't utter a single sound. I curled in the crook of her arm and waited for my body and my heart rate to return to normal. Neither of us spoke. I had enough energy to put my hand on her chest before I fell asleep, selfishly sated while Brynn waited.

❖

I woke some time before dawn. We were in the same position, only covered by a warm blanket. I wasn't cold, but I shivered anyway. Waking up next to a beautiful woman wasn't exactly something I was used to. Brynn's body was warm and I snuggled next to her, listening to the soft exhale of her breath near my ear. She was asleep, probably exhausted, since she did all of the work. I lay next to her for several minutes and enjoyed the feel of her body. I wanted to touch her everywhere, but I didn't think it was fair of me to wake her. I had been selfish for hours. I quietly slipped out of bed and headed to the bathroom to freshen up. A shower sounded heavenly so I closed the door and turned on the water. I wasn't wrong; the hot water felt amazing.

"It's kind of early, don't you think?" Brynn asked.

I gasped when Brynn opened the door to the shower. "You have to stop scaring me." I brushed the water from my eyes so I could properly see the tall, beautiful, and completely naked woman standing in front of me.

She reached for my hips and pushed me away from the stream to hog all the water. I couldn't keep my hands from touching her wet, slick body. "I'm six feet tall and walk like a Neanderthal. I'm not quiet," she said.

I poured soap on the bath sponge and reached out to her. She was stunning. There wasn't a single flaw on her body other than the tiny scar by her lip. "You're beautiful." I couldn't stay mad at her. Good things happened when she scared me. I was hoping for a repeat performance. Only this time, I wanted more of a leading role. She twirled me back under the water and gave me a proper good morning kiss.

"You're the beautiful one." She moaned when I lathered her breasts. I ran my thumbs over her nipples before I moved the sponge lower to rub between her legs. She leaned her head back under the water and tilted her body toward me. She was not afraid of pleasure, giving or receiving. She put her hands on the walls to brace herself and pushed down on my hand. I dropped the sponge and watched the water stream off of the muscles in her stomach and the junction of her thighs. I ran my hands over her.

When I dropped to my knees, she stood in front of the water so it wouldn't hit me. We made eye contact. She didn't look away. I ran my hands up her thighs and spread her apart. The water didn't deter me from the sweet target that I had been wanting for days. She wrapped her hands in my wet hair and drew me closer, gently bobbing my head against her as my tongue lavished her clit. Her power over me made me weak in such a phenomenal way. I submitted to her faster than I had to anyone else and, for the first time, I didn't care. I wanted to be in her control. Just as I was getting comfortable on my knees, she gently pulled me to my feet.

"Let's go back to bed. There's still a lot of time before I have to leave for work," she said.

I stood up, wrung out my hair, and reached for the towel she handed me. It took her thirty seconds to towel dry her entire body and her short hair. I was still struggling with drying off my body. I couldn't even figure out the tangled mess that was my hair.

There was no time for product or even to run a brush through it. Brynn tugged off my towel and walked me back to bed, touching me the entire time. I loved her hands on my body. I wanted to be greedy again, but I also had this desire to please her as much as she satisfied me.

"What time do you have to leave?" I managed to ask before her lips claimed mine.

We didn't talk for several minutes as we reacquainted ourselves under the covers. I worked my way over her body, nipping and kissing until I reached her warm, wet core. She was so ready for me and so patient over the last several hours. I didn't care if she was going to be late for work. This was the most important thing I was going to do today. I grabbed her thighs and pressed them open.

She held my wet, tousled hair back with one hand and lifted her hips to my mouth. I flattened my tongue against her slit and ran it up and down slowly until she bucked with pleasure. I sucked her clit into my mouth and swirled my fingertips along the inside of her thighs and down to her ass. Her moans encouraged me. I caressed the softness of her lips and carefully slid a finger inside of her. She was unbelievably tight. I moved my finger slowly and licked until her hips gyrated faster against me. The hand that was holding my hair up was now pressing my head into her. I loved it.

When she came, she was loud and her entire body shook with release. It was a beautiful sight. Her nipples were rock hard and a slight film of sweat glistened off of her chest and stomach. She pulled me into her arms and held me. My hair enveloped us when I finally stretched and kissed her.

"Looks like you won't be late after all." I placed tiny kisses across her face and on the sides of her neck until her breathing evened out.

"Who said we were done?" Brynn asked. She flipped me over and I forgot all about time as she continued her delicious discovery of my body until well after the sun came up.

CHAPTER NINETEEN

I decided to go with Brynn to the sanctuary. She offered and I wanted to be next to her. Spending more time there was on my agenda anyway. We never finished our tour of the place and I still had a ton of questions. Plus, we were both nervous about the men looking for me. I was mildly concerned at first, but with the fourth guy in the mix, I was looking over my shoulder every couple of minutes.

"You will definitely be safe at the sanctuary," Brynn said.

She said it more to herself, but I nodded. Rangers with guns. And they were all on my side. "Oh, I know," I said.

We didn't talk a lot as we were getting ready to finally start the day. Brynn kissed me a few times in the kitchen, but I could tell she was nervous. I hoped she wasn't regretting her decision. As if reading my mind, she reached over and held my hand. It was sweet and made me smile. I felt like I was in high school again.

We pulled into the parking lot and I jumped out of the truck, eager to see Wally again. I was thankful he wasn't at the cabin last night, but I missed him.

"How do you think he did last night?" I turned to Brynn before we reached the door. She reached out and cupped my chin. She didn't say anything, only stared at me and gave me a small, sad smile. I frowned. "Are you okay?" I touched her hand.

"I am. I think I'm just tired." She dropped her hand.

I reached out and grabbed it. I stepped closer to her and lowered my voice. "You hardly got any sleep last night."

She shrugged. "I got enough." She opened the door and we walked into the foyer. Wally scurried over to us.

"Wally!" I was so excited to see him. He waddled over to me first, surprising me.

"So that's how it's going to be, huh, my little man?" Brynn picked him up and flipped him onto his back. I reached out and tickled his stomach. He nipped at me, gently, like a puppy.

"Were you a good boy last night?" I asked.

"He got into just about everything, but I think he had a good time." Tina walked over to us and gave us a play by play of their night.

"Kennedy managed to lock herself out of the cabin and I found her wandering out behind it along the stream," Brynn said.

"My phone was sitting on the kitchen counter. I went outside to drink a cup of tea and shut the door without realizing it was locked," I said.

"Well, Brynn thought for sure the poachers found you. She shot out of here like a bullet when she couldn't reach you." Tina winked at Brynn and reached out to touch my arm. "We're glad you're okay."

I smiled at her. "Thank you. This is all a bit scary."

"I know waiting isn't easy, but I have faith that we'll catch them," Tina said. She excused herself to check on the animals in the back and Brynn went to her office to read a few reports and tuck Wally in. He needed a good nap since he didn't sleep at all at Tina's.

"Do you mind if I go visit with Tina for a few minutes? I want to see what she's doing today and maybe get a few more pics," I said.

Brynn's answer was a swift kiss on my lips. The kind that made me rethink my decision about leaving Brynn. "Go. Have fun. Learn something. I'll find you in a bit so we can head out."

I blew a kiss at Wally and trotted off after Tina. I picked the perfect time to show up as two rangers were bringing in a young bison whose leg was tangled in barbed wire. I didn't think. I grabbed my camera and clicked away. The rangers were trying hard to keep him from struggling and hurting himself further as they wrestled him off of the trailer.

"We couldn't get the wire off out in the field. It's in deep, Tina. I've given him one tranquilizer already." Rick, the hero who towed my car, was sweating profusely. His muscles were strained as he, Roger, and Brody, a ranger who jumped in to help, held the buffalo still while Tina administered another shot.

The buffalo fought the drug and eventually succumbed. They wasted no time as Tina called for assistance to help with the stitches. Rick carefully clipped off the wire and Tina went behind him, cleaning and suturing the injury. It was incredible to watch them work quietly, efficiently, and so in sync. After almost an hour of makeshift surgery right outside of the trailer, but still in the garage, the buffalo was stitched, bandaged, and dragged into a stall where he would have to spend some time to allow the sutures to heal. I was exhausted just watching all of them in action.

"Is it always like this? So chaotic and intense?" I asked. I looked around at four very tired and sweaty workers.

"Not to this degree, but yes. Whenever you deal with larger animals, it gets crazy because they aren't used to people or getting caught." The rangers nodded at Tina's assessment. "They think we're going to hurt them. A part of me believes they know deep down that we're helping, but we still keep our guards up."

I handed everybody a bottle of cold water from the break room, anxious to continue this unplanned interview. Tina's fresh, white, veterinarian jacket was covered in blood and ripped low where a barb caught the pocket during the take down. It was almost lunchtime and she still hadn't assessed the animals ready for release today. That would easily take the rest of the day even if she cut her lunch time in half.

"Why do you do what you do?" I asked her. A lot of people worked with animals, but usually the cute, fluffy kind. I was curious why this petite woman wasn't afraid to wrestle with some of the largest animals in Alaska.

"Every animal deserves a chance. Each one I work with has such a personality. It's amazing. The puffin from the other day? He struts around in his cage cackling at all the animals. And the elk? Do you remember him? He's scared of his own shadow, but in a playful way. It's almost as if he laughs at himself. You know Wally and what a delight he is."

What she said was true. People liked to have pets, but what these people were doing here, was far greater and less selfish than pet ownership. "It must be hard to form a bond and then have to release it back into the wild." I sat while Tina cleaned up. She had several white coats hanging in a locker so this clearly happened a lot.

"Yes, but it's still so satisfying knowing that we've extended the life of one of these majestic creatures. Plus, I get to handle so many different animals that most vets don't get to. Brynn probably mentioned that I worked in a regular practice before I was able to come here full-time. I enjoyed that work, but this is fulfilling in a very different way." She smoothed out the front of her clean coat after she buttoned it. "Are you ready to make the rounds?"

I followed her into the first room that housed smaller animals. They were all separated by diets. The herbivores were in one room, the carnivores in another. Larger animals had their own bays to heal in.

"What percentage of the animals get released and live to have long, healthy lives?"

Tina sighed. "Well, the circle of life is alive and well in Alaska. It's heartbreaking when we heal an animal and set it free, only to find a wolf or another animal killed it a few days or weeks later."

"How do you know it's one you've treated? By the scars?" I was genuinely curious.

"We tag them before they leave. It helps us understand so much about migration, population, and just their behavior as a whole." She handed me a stainless steel disc that was smaller than a dime. "This is the largest one we have. It stores their information and serves as a tracker, too."

"These have to cost some serious money. How are you paying for all of this?" The sanctuary was nice and clean, but nothing showy.

"We always struggle. Everyone here spends their downtime filling out paperwork for grants to make up for the gap between our federal funding and our operational costs. Most of our visitors donate. A few dollars here and there help. We receive donations from wealthy patrons and the sanctuary has fundraisers to increase awareness and interest," she said.

"I think what you do here's incredible. Were you born in Alaska or did you move here?" I asked.

"My father was in the military and we were stationed in Fairbanks for all of my high school years. When he got transferred, I stayed. I always knew I was going to work with animals. I just didn't expect they would be the kind that weighed more than me." Tina put her finger to her lips and signaled to me to be quiet. We tiptoed into a room where there were two tiny, sleepy bobcats. She slipped on gloves and signaled that I should do the same.

I put my camera and notepad on the counter so I could put on the gloves. I had no idea why, but my heart was racing. I figured she was only going to let me touch one, but when she handed me a kitten, I almost died. I carefully held the tiny animal close to my chest. The baby was so sleepy that she opened her tiny blue eyes for just a second, saw me, and curled up back into my hand and drifted back to sleep.

"We need to feed them. Do you want to help?" she asked.

I nodded. She handed me the second kitten who was a little bit more awake, while she fixed two bottles. I stood there as awkward as could be, and held these tiny bundles of wilderness. "What happened to them? Why are they here?" My whisper was horribly loud. It was too hard to contain my excitement. "They seem fine."

"They are. One of the rangers found them after their mother died," Tina said. She didn't elaborate on the mother's death, and I didn't ask. It made me sad.

"And they are too young to make it out on their own. Will they be released ever?" I asked.

"It depends, but they will probably stay at the sanctuary. When animals this young come to us, the chances of them surviving out in the wilderness are slim."

I frowned and held their sleeping faces in front of mine. "They are so cute. And they look like normal kittens except for their goatees."

Tina handed me a tiny bottle and took one of the kittens back. When the kitten latched on to the nipple, his little ears started moving back and forth as he greedily drank from it. I couldn't wait to feed mine. I rubbed the bottle's soft nipple on her mouth until she latched on. She made tiny squeals and reached her paws out to capture my hands to ensure I wasn't going to leave.

"How often do you have to feed them?" I asked.

"Every three hours. This is the second time since I've been here." After about ten minutes, both kittens passed out with milk mustaches and full bellies. Tina snapped a few pictures of me feeding the kitten after she put hers back in the pen. I couldn't wait to see the photos.

"Are you ready for lunch?" Brynn walked in and quieted after I shushed her.

"Don't wake the babies. We just got them to sleep," I said.

She smiled at me and nodded. "Are you hungry?" she whispered. I nodded. "Want to grab a late lunch?"

I regretfully handed the kitten back to Tina. "Thank you so much for letting me spend my morning here."

"Anytime, Kennedy. It's nice to talk about our little place with somebody who can make a difference."

Chapter Twenty

Brynn and I decided on Lucille's for lunch. It was my favorite spot in town. We ran into Mandy while eating meatloaf specials.

"Would you and Lisa like to come over to the cabin for dinner tonight?" Brynn asked.

"That sounds great. I'm tired of cooking," Mandy said.

We decided on six. Brynn and I were responsible for the sides, they would bring the fish. I smiled because it felt like Brynn and I were a couple. At least at this moment.

"You know, if I keep eating like this, I'm not going to fit in my clothes." I shoveled another forkful of mashed potatoes into my mouth.

"You're perfect. Don't even worry about it," Brynn said.

I smiled as I recalled the last twelve hours of my life. I finally had sex with Brynn and it was even better than I imagined. I witnessed a beautiful rescue at the sanctuary, and bottle fed a baby bobcat. And the sexiest woman in the room just told me I was perfect.

"Thank you. As you can tell, I'm not too worried about my calories today," I said.

"You did burn off quite a few of them earlier," she said. I blushed and looked at my plate. "Thank you for last night. Or this morning, I mean." I looked at her smiling face. I didn't see regret or remorse, only happiness. It was different than the sad smile she gave me just this morning.

"Are you okay with everything? I mean, I know you didn't…"
I trailed off hoping she wouldn't need any more of an explanation.
She reached across the table and held my hand. "I'm fine. I
promise. It was fantastic."

I was still sore from this morning, but I wanted her again. "I
know that you had reservations about starting anything with me
and I just want you to know that I respect you." That sounded lame
even to me. "What I mean is thank you, too."

"Are you ready?" Brynn asked. She paid the bill, and we
headed back to the sanctuary. She promised me more time inside
the fences which translated to private time where we could kiss
and be alone again.

❖

"So tell me something you can't do."

Brynn pulled over to repair a busted fence near the road.
The tailgate on the truck was down and served as my seat while I
handed her the tools she needed. I didn't know a crescent wrench
from needle nose pliers, so she had to work with me on a different
level. "Hand me the rubber grip things that look like a red dolphin"
or "grab me the yellow handle cross screw driver." I was worthless.
I knew what a hammer was, but that was the extent of my tool
knowledge.

"Oh, let's see, I can't write well. I can't fit into small spaces.
Oh, and I can't seem to get you off of my mind." She smiled.

That made my stomach flutter. "Brynn Coleman. You're a
flirt."

She winked at me and continued hammering the spike into
the post. The sun was beating down on her and her ranger hat only
shielded half her face. I took a picture of her and the vastness of
the mountains around us. I could photograph her all day.

"I'm horrible at flirting," she said.

I handed her a drink in exchange for the red dolphin thing.
"Shut up." I stared at her in disbelief.

She laughed and a little dribble of water escaped her mouth. "What?" she asked innocently.

"At first I thought you were a bad flirt, but then you turned on your charm and bam, I ended up naked on your couch." I pulled her close to me and tilted her hat back. Sitting on the tailgate gave me additional height and I was able to look her in the eye.

"My couch will never be the same," she said.

"I will never be the same."

She cleared her throat and took a step back. Fuck. I said the wrong thing.

"Let me gather the rest of the supplies and we'll get going." She turned her back to me and checked her work on the post. I sighed and jumped down. Tender moment ruined. Great job, Kennedy.

Brynn kept the conversation light during our drive to the western side of the refuge. The river that cut in front of the mountain provided water for the animals and we saw our fair share of elk and moose. I had a hard time distinguishing between female elk and female moose and it eventually became a game with us. I blamed our distance and my eyesight. Brynn blamed my lack of interest in animals. It was nice that she was loose around me again. I vowed not to discuss our relationship, however brief it would be, until she wanted to.

"We should probably get out of here and hit the grocery store so we don't miss Mandy and Lisa," Brynn said.

"I'm excited to see them again. They are both sweet ladies." I thought about my friends back home and how I really didn't have any couple friends. My friends were single and only cared about going to bars and hooking up. Dinner at my condo just didn't happen ever. I was looking forward to spending time with three people I genuinely liked.

"We have our spurts. Now that it's spring, we'll get out more and do fun things like softball and movie nights," she said. We pulled into the parking lot and I helped Brynn transfer her things back into her truck.

"Like everybody meet at the theater or the drive-in?" It seemed pretty obvious to me, but it was just a different world here in Alaska.

"We don't have drive-in theaters. It doesn't get dark enough during the summer to show movies outside, and it's just too cold the rest of the year. Somebody from the softball team will have a movie party at their house. It's fun."

It did sound fun. Simple, but fun. I rarely went to movies, but when I did, it was usually a red carpet event and then I spent more time watching the audience than the movie. I couldn't recall the last movie I saw for fun. "What's your favorite movie?"

"Oh, I couldn't even narrow it down. I spend a lot of time in front of the television watching cheesy eighties movies, historical pieces, science fiction, and documentaries. I love them all." She never turned on the television at the cabin. I told myself to be a better guest there and engage her in conversation, since she gave me her undivided attention and I didn't even know it.

"What are winters like here? Are they as brutal as I imagine?" I asked.

"Hold that thought. I'm going to run in, grab Wally, and check out. Do you want to come in or stay in the car?" I checked the time. It was already five and we still had to go shopping.

"It will be quicker if I stay." She leaned over and kissed me swiftly before heading inside. I held my fingertips to my lips to keep the kiss just a few seconds longer.

When Brynn kissed me in front of Mandy and Lisa, I nearly swooned. I acted like it was no big thing, but I didn't miss the look shared between them.

"How much longer on the fish? Do you need my help?" Lisa asked.

Brynn snapped her tongs at her. "Grilling's my thing. You sit next to your wife and look pretty." When she walked outside to check on the fish, both women looked at me. Mandy had a huge smile on her face, and Lisa looked like she was chomping at the bit to ask questions. Mandy reached over and gently squeezed Lisa's forearm.

I held up my hands to them in a surrendering gesture. "What can I say? She's charming." I shrugged at them as if it was no big deal, but we all knew it was. I stole a moment to watch Brynn in action. The spring breeze ruffled her hair and turned up the collar of her shirt. I pictured myself standing next to her, brushing it down just to have an excuse to touch her. Her hair was so thick, and dark, and I longed to dig my fingers in it again like I did the night before.

"She's like a unicorn," Lisa whispered. I busted out laughing. Brynn looked in at us.

I shrugged at her and turned back to the girls. "What exactly do you mean?"

"We've known Brynn a long time and haven't seen her with anybody really. Well, not cutesy like this. It's nice to see," Mandy said.

I smiled, but it felt bittersweet. "Brynn and I know this isn't going to be anything other than right here, right now. I'll probably leave next week. My articles are almost done. I just need to fine tune them and send them in."

"What happens to you and Brynn?" Lisa asked.

Before I had a chance to answer, Brynn walked in with a platter of grilled halibut. "Why do I get the feeling you ladies are talking about me?" She set the fish in the center of the table and we all leaned forward to look at it in appreciation.

"This smells wonderful, Brynn," Mandy said. Plates were passed around, sides were dished out, and two minutes later, we were all eating a delicious and healthy meal, my favorite yet.

"It tastes even better than it smells," I said.

"Brynn, I might need your recipe so that I can share this deliciousness with the diner," Mandy said. She listed off possible ingredients, but Brynn shook her head.

"No way. What happens if I want to open a diner and nobody comes to my place because they are over at Lucille's. I got to keep my options open."

"You could never quit your job. You love it too much," Lisa said.

Brynn nodded. "This is true." She told Mandy all of the herbs and spices she used.

Lisa and I shrugged at one another. "Women," she said.

"I know nothing about cooking," I said.

"What do you eat when you are home?"

"Usually just salads and simple foods like yogurt and avocados. Nothing that requires heat other than from a microwave," I said.

"Seriously? You never got the bug to cook? What about cooking for anyone?" Mandy seemed amazed that somebody could be my age and know zero about cooking. I wasn't proud that I didn't know how long to boil an egg for, but I wasn't embarrassed either. It just wasn't my thing.

"I live near a lot of restaurants. It's handy to run to the corner and pick up something fast and healthy. Truthfully, it's just hard to cook just for one person."

"I like to cook. When you are snowed in, you learn ways to entertain yourself. Cooking was mine," Brynn said.

"You're great at it. Brynn has cooked some pretty amazing things for me over the last few days. This is probably my favorite." I turned to Mandy and Lisa. "And both of you have strong family backgrounds in food." Mandy grew up helping her mother at Lucille's, while Lisa's family specialized in smoking fish. Even though they didn't have a restaurant, they sold cookbooks of family recipes gathered throughout the years.

"My mother's a horrible cook. I learned my skills from her." Everybody laughed even though I was serious. "We usually ate one thing only. Like meatloaf. What's for dinner, mom? A slice of meatloaf. Not nestled on a bed of soft and fluffy mashed potatoes resting near a pile of sweet peas and a dinner roll, but a slice of meatloaf smothered in ketchup."

"Seriously? Is that why you're so thin?" Lisa asked.

"No. That's because I work in an industry where you have to be a size two in order to succeed. It's tough. I'm going to blame

Mandy, though, for making me fall off of the wagon. That fish I had at Lucille's was buttery and so delicious." I took a break from talking so I could eat. My clothes still fit even though I had forgotten about calories for two weeks so I planned on savoring every bite. I felt Brynn's hand on my knee and smiled. She wasn't being secretive or coy, she was being sweet and supportive. It was nice to be on the receiving end of her attention. I felt oddly at peace and excited at the same time.

"My mother has a way of making you forget about diets and calorie counting," Mandy said.

"I'm already in love with her." I laughed at my own joke. I was completely relaxed around these women. They were down-to-earth. I wasn't used to genuine people and wondered why. Why did I surround myself with people who gossiped instead of talked? Or ridiculed instead of complimented? How had I never realized I was in unhealthy relationships?

We took our glasses of wine and relaxed in the living room. I sat next to Brynn, our bodies touching from shoulders to knees, her arm draped on the sofa behind me. Mandy sat on my other side, and Lisa sat in the chair across from the three of us. Wally was in the corner playing with a baby mobile that Brynn raccoon-proofed for him. A lot of our conversation revolved around him. I was amazed at how much Mandy and Lisa knew about raccoons. I would google raccoons as pets later. According to everyone, small animals were not recommended as pets because they were potential prey. Not just of coyotes, wolves, and large cats on the ground, but animals from above. Eagles, hawks, and other large birds were always around watching and waiting. If you had a small animal as a pet and wanted to keep it, you had to be around it when you let it outside for whatever reason. Brynn was worried about Wally, but he didn't get out much unless he was surrounded by rangers at the sanctuary or Brynn at the cabin. He stayed pretty close to the people he trusted. I realized I was doing the exact same thing.

CHAPTER TWENTY-ONE

Brynn put her fingertips on the top of the doorframe and leaned forward as we watched Mandy and Lisa drive away. The gentle sway of her lithe body near mine gave me a surge of energy I wasn't expecting. I was tired and desperately needed sleep, but the need to touch her again outweighed that need.

"Even though it's still early and as much as I like them, I thought they would never leave," Brynn said. Her hand slid to my waist and gently pulled me closer. It was nice to be held.

"I know. I'm exhausted," I said.

She tilted my chin so that she could look into my eyes. "Too tired for me?" There was such vulnerability in her voice. Even the tiny, soft kiss she placed on my lips was cautious. Gone was the confident woman who laughed and joked with us just a few minutes ago.

"Never too tired for you." I stood on my toes and kissed her, softly at first, but our passion quickly surfaced and it was just a matter of moments before we both started taking off our clothes. I was anxious to touch her and feel her muscles bunch and quiver under my fingertips. This morning was rushed with desperate need to satisfy our lust for one another. Tonight, I wanted it to be slower and sweeter. Brynn broke our kiss first.

"We should probably go inside." She was great about making me forget everything else around me. I stood out on the porch with my shirt unbuttoned and my jeans down past my hips. Brynn was in about the same state. She pushed us back inside the cabin and locked the front door. Wally was in the kitchen eating grapes. We barely acknowledged him on our way to the bedroom. Brynn shut the door and reached for me.

I stepped out of my jeans and pulled off my shirt before I went into her arms. Tonight we had time. "Even though we had fun with them, I like that it's just us," I said.

She answered me with a kiss that made me so weak I had to sit. Her mouth was incredible. Brynn gave all of herself in each and every kiss. There was a meaning behind each one: I want you, I need you, I trust you. I sat on the edge of the bed and pulled her close. Her jeans were unbuttoned and hanging low on her sharp hips. I pressed my palms on her smooth stomach and slid them inside of the opening of her jeans to push them down. Her body was so soft that I had to run my fingertips over her skin several times because I couldn't believe what I felt. She moaned and stepped closer between my legs. I kissed her stomach and finished pushing her jeans down. She smelled warm, and wet, and ready for me. I rubbed my fingers along the seam of her boxers, the one that ran up and down her slit. She pressed into me, gently at first. Her fingers wound in my hair and drew me closer.

"You taste so sweet." I licked the tiny, almost invisible hairs nestled between her belly button and the waistband of her boxers. I pulled the boxers down and placed tiny kisses along an imaginary trail to her clit.

Brynn gasped when I found the hard spot and I ran my tongue gently over it, around it, savoring it. She shook off her shirt and stripped off her sports bra. She wasn't nervous or ashamed of being naked. She was glorious. Six feet tall and lean, smooth, and sexy. I was going to take my time with her. I pulled her onto the bed with me and stretched her out so that I could touch her everywhere.

"You feel so good against me," she said.

I straddled her and ran my hands over her arms, across her shoulders, and up her neck. When I leaned to kiss her, she held my head and slipped her tongue past my lips. I moaned when her tongue stroked mine. I had never been so thoroughly kissed before. It was heavenly. She ran her hands up my thighs to tug at my panties. Without breaking the kiss, I leaned up and kicked them off. She unclasped my bra and I sank down onto her heat, relishing her bare skin against mine. Her body was hard, yet soft in the right places. Her small breasts were firm, sensitive, and I finally broke the kiss to take one of her nipples into my mouth. She bucked her hips beneath me and gave a groan of approval. I moved to the other breast and gave it the same attention. Her body tensed and she flipped me so she was nestled between my legs. I wrapped my thighs around her waist and she moaned into my ear.

"You are so wet." She ground her hips into mine and made me even wetter. She slipped her hand between us and easily slid two fingers inside me. I forgot about everything at that moment except her. I wiggled my hips and pushed into each thrust, welcoming the pleasurable pain of her depth. She stopped just as I was climbing my way to a fantastic orgasm. I groaned in disappointment when she stopped her thrusts.

I gasped. "What's wrong?"

Her shoulders glistened with a thin sheen of sweat. I leaned up and licked her collarbone after scraping my teeth on her shoulder. She kissed me before answering. "I want you to come in my mouth. I love feeling you let go that way."

I wasn't going to say no. She was extremely talented with her mouth and her hands. It would only be a matter of seconds no matter how hard I tried not to come. She kissed her way down my body and picked up her thrusts when her mouth found my clit. I grabbed the pillow next to me and squeezed it close to my body, picturing her still in my arms. When my legs started to shake, her fingers pushed even deeper inside me. I came loudly, knowing that nobody could hear me for miles. I stopped her because I couldn't take anymore.

"I just can't," I said.

She climbed up my body and kissed me like she had previously. I melted. I couldn't move. When Brynn Coleman made love to a woman, she gave one hundred percent.

"I love listening to you when you come." She moved to my side and stroked my skin as I relaxed. Leaning on her elbow, she looked at me, a smug smile on her gorgeous face.

"You look rather pleased with yourself." I touched her cheek, running my fingertip over her full lips and pressing lightly. She playfully placed a kiss on the tip, which I brought to my mouth.

"Guilty." She resumed touching me. I was working up the energy to touch her back, but she was making it difficult. When her hands were on my body, I thought of little else.

"If you don't stop, I'm never going to get the chance to return the favor," I said. At least that's what I hoped I said. What actually came out was probably more like a moan here and there, punctuated with syllables that resembled those words.

"Like I could stop you."

"What do you mean by that?" I asked.

"Are you kidding? You are the most tenacious woman I've ever met. I mean that in a good way. Even though it's been so rough for you here and you've had the worst luck of any other person I've ever known, you haven't stopped. You've adjusted, and moved forward. Every single time. It's fantastic."

I kissed her because it was nice to be recognized the way I wanted to be. I also wanted her to know that in just the few short weeks I'd known her, she'd changed the way I saw myself and the rest of the world, but I didn't know how to say that without getting mushy. This relationship was only supposed to be fun and flirty, not heavy and emotional. I pasted on a smile and pushed her back on the mattress.

"Mmm, this is nice," she said.

I pushed her legs apart with my knees and placed kisses all the way down her body until I hit the juncture of her thighs. She was still wet. I spread her apart with my hands and savored her with my mouth. "So warm," I said against her pussy. I ran my tongue from the bottom of her slit all the way up to her clit.

When I dabbed my tongue on the soft skin just below her opening, she moaned loudly but didn't stop me. Her hips jerked toward my mouth. When I felt her hands on the back of my head, I knew she was serious. I moved my mouth up and concentrated on her engorged clit. I held her hips and licked and sucked until she came gloriously.

"You even come beautifully." I climbed up her body and kissed her again. "At some point, you're going to let me go first. Contrary to popular belief, I'm really not a pillow princess."

Brynn laughed even though it was difficult for her to catch her breath. "I never once thought that. I just can't keep my hands off of you. Once you start touching me, I have to have you," she said.

I kissed her shoulder and the soft spot right above her heart before I thought about what I was doing. When I looked at her, she raised her eyebrow at me. I ignored her and tried to come up with anything to talk about to get out of the awkward situation. Since when was I romantic?

"You always say the right things. I think you're perfect."

She laughed. "I'm far from it." She lazily twirled my hair through her fingers.

"You know, I'm never wrong. I might be a complete wreck here, but in the lower forty-eight," I put air quotes around lower forty-eight, "I have my shit together. I can read people pretty well and you, Brynn Coleman, are pretty amazing."

She shrugged. "I certainly have flaws and I'm a pretty simple person. There's not much to me other than what you already know."

"Wait. I know your flaw. This tiny scar near your lip." I traced it with my fingertip until she playfully bit my finger. "It's hideous."

"I frighten children in town with this face." She played along. "That's why I work out in nature so I can hide with the animals. They accept me for who I am."

"You're beautiful inside and out. I want to know more though. Tell me something I don't know about you."

"You think I'm amazing, but I'm damaged goods." She rested her head on my shoulder so I couldn't read her expression. I rubbed the back of her head.

"You're not damaged at all. I don't know why you'd think that," I said.

"My history's awful."

"You know, if you want to talk about it, I'm here. This is a judgment free zone. You already know how unsavory my history is." Brynn hadn't thought any less of me when I told her my story. "And yet when I told you, you didn't bat an eye. I'm certainly not going to hold anything you tell me against you. I might be somewhat of a snob, but I do care about you."

"You're right. I should trust you more. You've been nothing but sweet to me." She sighed.

I felt her hesitation and treaded lightly. "If you aren't comfortable, I understand. I don't want to push you or make you feel like you have to tell me about it." I held her for a few moments and enjoyed the feeling of her weight on half my body. I smiled because we fit well.

"Remember when I told you that my girlfriend cheated on me?" She felt me nod and continued. "Tiffany. We met in high school when she transferred from North Carolina. She made the team and at first we were at each other's throats vying for the top spot."

"I can't imagine you being competitive. How did you go from enemies to girlfriends? What was the attraction?" I asked.

"She was fresh and exciting and beautiful. I didn't mind her flaws. They made her more interesting. Looking back, she always wanted the best. I dropped everything in my life to cater to hers. She was selfish and a little cruel. I overlooked it because her home life wasn't great and I chalked it up to her covering up her own unhappiness."

I felt Brynn's breath on my neck as she sighed heavily. "I already hate her." I gave her a tight squeeze. I felt her smile against my skin.

"I knew I was going to Florida State, regardless. My dad was an assistant coach there, I practiced at their pool, and I was friends with all the girls there." Her voice relaxed as she told the story. It was like she had told it before, but never out loud. "Tiffany got a scholarship to attend, too, and my dad helped both of us train.

We were great together. Top swimmers, fantastic lovers, sweet girlfriends."

"So how long did you date including the time together in high school?" I was curious because first loves were damaging. It was hard to protect your heart if you didn't know how hard it could fall.

"All together? About three years. It was great. We were in love, not afraid to be out. My parents weren't waving rainbow flags or anything, but they didn't deter our relationship. Well, until we got to Florida State. Then my dad started getting agitated and told us we weren't supposed to cling to one another in public. We were representing the school and were to behave ourselves."

"How did you handle that? I'm sure it was hard to be the coach's daughter. But college? Come on. That's the time when the real world doesn't matter. Nobody judges in college."

"Oh, yes they do." She snorted sarcastically. "Tiffany became distant with me. I could feel her slipping away, but I wasn't sure why. I went to practice early one day to have a heart to heart with my dad. I couldn't take her shutting me out any longer and I thought it had to do with how he was treating us. When I went to his office, I knocked first, but walked in because hey, I'm his daughter. What could he possibly want to hide from me?"

I felt her tense and I held her tighter. I imagined the worst-case scenario because that was how my mind worked. "It's okay, Brynn. It's okay." Those are only words that people say when nothing else will do. She grew quiet and I stroked her back for a few seconds.

"Yeah, so I walk in to find my dad banging my girlfriend. My girlfriend. I stood in the doorway in complete disbelief. My dad yelled at me to get out and my girlfriend, well, ex-girlfriend, started crying. I was in shock."

"Oh, my God. That's horrible. I'm so sorry they hurt you like that," I said. Yes, I'd slept with someone married, too, but I believed Nikki's marriage was over. The fact that it was Brynn's father made the affair much worse.

"Eventually, it got out. Instead of being mad at my dad for having an affair with another woman, I got blamed. She was my girlfriend and I had paraded her around our house for years in just a bikini and why wouldn't my father be tempted? My mother sided with him. I was the bad guy for allowing it to happen." Brynn sounded dejected.

I wondered if this was the first time she talked about this to another person. "I'm sorry, Brynn. I'm sorry your family rejected you and hurt you like that."

She lifted her head and stared into my eyes. "Now you know why it's so hard for me to trust people."

I stroked her chin. "I'm not her. I'm not nineteen. I'm high maintenance, yes, but I'm nothing like Tiffany. Your parents are assholes. Their reaction would destroy anyone's ability to trust. I'm glad you got away from them. Alaska's kind of extreme, but I get it. I do." I didn't ask her about why she changed her last name. She would tell me on her own time.

"Last I heard, my mom kicked my dad out after Tiffany got pregnant. So I might have a half sibling that I know nothing about. That's what makes me the asshole. I haven't tried to find them."

"You're not an asshole. Your situation is completely unique. It's hard right now to make the effort. Maybe when your sibling is old enough, they can try to reach out to you. I'm sure one day they will be able to appreciate the tough situation you're in." I wanted her to know that it wasn't up to her. I doubted the family would be willing to let Brynn in their lives. People had a weird way of skewing the truth to help them sleep better at night. I trusted Brynn. I believed her story and I understood why it was so hard for her to share.

"It's such an awkward situation and it's not the kid's fault. They are probably telling them all sorts of lies about me. That's what gets me. I did nothing wrong except fall in love with a jerk."

I rubbed her back, not sorry I asked, but sad that our tender moment was gone. I pulled the blanket over us. "So you haven't spoken to your family in ten years?" I certainly wasn't close to my family, but I called home once a month.

"Not a single word. I moved here, changed my name, and pretended not to have a past," she said.

Bingo. "Your last name isn't Coleman?" At least I no longer had to pretend I didn't know.

"Now it is. I had it legally changed to my grandmother's maiden name several years ago. I wanted nothing to do with the Whitfield family name and I was close to my grandmother on my mother's side. When she died, I inherited a little bit of money and invested in some property."

"You've done an amazing thing here. Your place, your job. You. You should be proud of yourself." When I was nineteen, I worried about things like my wardrobe and getting into parties even though I was too young to drink. I thought Brynn was brave for leaving at such a young age and never looking back. I held her close and rubbed her back until she fell asleep in my arms. It was nice to be in charge of another person. For the first time, maybe ever, I felt content.

CHAPTER TWENTY-TWO

"Hello?" Brynn answered her phone. What the hell time was it? The light coming in the window was faint, but morning was just over the horizon. "Yeah, no, I'm awake, Lara. What's going on?"

She sat on the edge of the mattress. I reached out and put my hand on her back. I liked touching her to let her know I was close. I heard Lara talk, but I couldn't make out her words. I rolled toward Brynn and placed tiny kisses on her spine while she carried on her conversation.

"He actually showed up there? Well, I'm glad the kid had enough sense to talk to him. I don't want him hurt just for a silly confidentiality agreement. No civilian job is worth that," Brynn said.

That got me to sit up. I leaned against her back and listened to what Lara was saying.

"He looked in his computer and told the guy exactly what he thought was the truth. Then he told his boss and his boss told him to call us. Good job on making it seem as if Kennedy was gone," Lara said.

"Did the kid get a good look at him? Do we have a good description of him?" Brynn asked.

"Even better. We have video."

Even though her voice was muffled, I heard it. They had a picture of the mysterious fourth man. According to Lara, it sounded as if he was the same man who visited Cee a few days ago, though they would need to wait until later in the morning to confirm. For some reason, this group was hell bent on finding me. When Brynn finally hung up, I fell back on the bed and looked at her.

"Seriously, what is the worst thing that could happen to a poacher here in Alaska? A fine? Have his license taken away? Why are these hunters after me?" I was getting worried.

"These guys are too organized and driven to be common poachers. So if this is as big as we think it is, we're talking jail time. Yes, fines and all of that, but depending on what Lara and her people are able to find when they arrest these guys, they could go away for a long time." Brynn explained how just recently, they locked up a guy for almost three years for shooting a bear cub on government land. "A lot of hunting is trust. We trust that hunters are following the rules and leave it to them to determine if the animal they are thinking about shooting is eligible and if they are going to report it. We only catch a few of the many who break the rules, so the ones we do catch, we make examples out of." She slid back under the blanket and pulled me close to her. I felt protected in her arms.

"Do we have to get up?" I asked. I kissed the skin closest to my mouth, which happened to be her neck.

She laughed softly. "No. We can sleep for a little bit longer." She squeezed me and kissed the top of my head.

"What if I don't want to sleep?"

"Your appetite is insatiable, woman."

We didn't talk for at least another hour.

"I don't understand why you won't let me stay here. You were fine with it earlier." We were finally up and dressed. I wanted to stay behind and write, but Brynn wanted me next to her.

"I would feel better if you were with me." She fixed her coffee and poured it in her travel mug. Wally was in the kitchen scurrying around Brynn's legs. He was excited to go. I wasn't.

"We've been through this before. Nobody on Earth knows I'm here. I'm the safest in this cabin. I can't even get locked out anymore. I'm so close to finishing my articles. Please, Brynn. You have to trust me. If there is a problem, you will be the first person I call. I promise." I slid my arms around her waist and kissed her neck. She remained stoic until she felt my tongue on her skin. I felt her relax and give in.

"Okay, but wear clothes with pockets so you can hear your phone if I call," she said.

"You're so bossy," I said, but I nodded. She had caved and I won.

"Look, I'm not trying to tell you how to live your life. I'm just worried. I…care for you. I really do. We have a good thing going. I feel responsible for you." She pulled me close to her and kissed me soundly on the mouth. "And I mean that in a good way, not a possessive way."

"I know. You've been wonderful to me. I don't want anything to happen to me either." I bent down and picked up Wally. For the first time ever, he let me. He liked to be flipped on his back so I carried him like a baby and followed Brynn out to the truck.

"Here are the keys to the Toyota. If you need anything, take it. Just please let me know you're out and about so I don't freak." She crawled into her truck and took Wally from me. He scurried to the passenger side and leaned up on the dash.

"Should he be put in a seat belt?"

Brynn laughed. "Sure, go ahead. Try to restrain a wild animal."

"Or at least a cage so if you hit something, he doesn't get hurt?" I was starting to care for more than just Brynn.

"He'll be fine. I promise. Go finish your story. I'll check in with you later." She leaned down and kissed me. It was sweet and so couple-like. I almost bounced away, but then realized I was an adult so I stood there and waved as she drove off. Then I bounced up the stairs and into the cabin.

I wanted to review the fishing story and get words down on the sanctuary, but I also wanted to finish my memoirs of my time here. I pulled up my photo folder labeled "Sanctuary" and looked through all of the photos. I had some incredible shots. I grabbed a cup of coffee, locked the cabin door, and sat down to get caught up on my experiences.

Brynn's call scared the living shit out of me. I fumbled to answer the call. "Hi." Four hours had passed. I'd barely looked up from my computer during that time. I took off my glasses and rubbed the bridge of my nose. My eyes were scratchy and I wasn't blinking enough. Time for a break.

"How's it going?" Her voice sounded strained.

"Good. What's going on with you? Why do you sound upset?"

"Just received some news. Lara called to tell me the troopers found one of the trailers you took photos of on a back road."

"Did they find anything in it?" I was anxious for her answer.

"Well, the truck was beat to hell. Somebody took a bat to it, smashed out all of the windows, and ripped up the seats."

"I'm surprised they didn't set it on fire." In my mind, that was the quickest way to get rid of evidence.

"The smoke would draw too much attention. They ripped out all of the tags and scratched out all serial plates on the truck, but they missed a tag on the trailer." She didn't sound excited about that information. My heart sank.

"They couldn't find anything on it?"

"The trailer was registered to a company that doesn't exist anymore so they are running every name they can find associated with the company through the database. They've set a trap if the owners come back, but at this point, it's obvious they abandoned them."

"Wow. Who can afford to just leave a giant truck and trailer behind?" Between the two of them, those items must have cost about a hundred grand.

"Hunters who are doing illegal stuff for high profits, that's who."

"Brynn, they'll catch these guys." I sounded sure and positive, but I was surprised they were still in the area. I would have been in a different time zone by now.

"I know. I'm just worried. I want them gone so that you and all of the animals are okay. We haven't had a poaching problem this close to town in a long time." Her tone was scaring me.

"Seriously, I can't imagine they would hurt me." My voice shook. I cleared my throat, determined to sound strong and sure. "Hunting big game illegally is one thing, murder is a whole different ballgame. Nobody wants to go to jail over me."

"We don't know what they are capable of. People change when it comes to large amounts of money. We have no idea how big this poaching ring is." Her voice was muffled and I pictured her running her hands over her face. I almost smiled at the visual. I had to change the subject for both of our sakes.

"I'm holed up in your fortress. Nobody knows I'm here. Let's assume they aren't even going to find me. Okay? Thank you for calling me and letting me know. Let's talk about something else. Tell me about your day. How's Wally?" Brynn was overthinking all of this. I wasn't the best thing to happen to her with all of my mishaps and crappy attitude. She, however, was the best thing to happen to me.

"Wally's out there greeting people. Fishing season starts in a few weeks so people are starting to trickle in. That's good for the sanctuary. We'll start getting donations and can get things we need like equipment, medicine, and cages," she said.

We chatted for about five more minutes. I talked her out of coming home for a late lunch. I was on a roll and only wanted to stop to eat a bite. I didn't want to have to entertain. I loved that she understood and kept her distance. Brynn Coleman was perfect for me and my career.

CHAPTER TWENTY-THREE

"A t some point, you're going to have to turn in something." I rolled my eyes while Erin chewed me out.

"I promise you will have everything tomorrow," I said. The fishing story was done and I was polishing it up when she called, surprising me.

"When are you coming back?"

I was quiet as I thought about her question. I hadn't thought about going home since day two of my trip here. Even with poachers looking for me, I was having a good time. No, I was having the time of my life. I met some great people, ate fantastic food, and had sex almost every night with a beautiful butch. Brynn was amazing. Not just in the bedroom, but with everything she did. She didn't take shortcuts and approached life head-on.

"Soon. After I send everything to you, I would like you to read it and let me know if there's anything else we need while I'm still here. You know, pictures, waivers, that kind of thing." It sounded like a good excuse. I hoped she would fall for it.

"How is everything else going? Are you staying out of trouble?" she asked.

Shit. I forgot to tell her about the poaching thing. "About that," I said.

"You've got to be kidding me, Kennedy. Did you trash another car?" She groaned.

I sat and told her the whole story from the animal that got shot, to the mysterious man looking for me at the car rental place. "How can nobody know that guy? Surely they have facial recognition software they can use," Erin said. I pictured her sitting on the edge of her seat, leaning forward, eating popcorn, listening to every single word like it was my last.

"It's not as if Anchorage's police force has FBI equipment. This whole town seems pretty low key. No frills. Besides, it's only been a week. They will get these guys," I said.

"A week?" She practically shouted it. "That's it. Get back here."

My heart sank. I wasn't ready to go home. There were too many unfinished things, words, feelings here in Alaska. "I can't. They might need me to identify these guys or whatever. I'll stay here for a few more days and wrap things up. I'll be in next week to discuss my first assignment back on *Mainstream*."

She snorted. "Yeah, let me read your feature first. Then we can discuss your next move."

"Don't even think about backing out. We have an agreement. Signed even." My voice got higher.

"Relax. I'm just playing with you. I'm sure your article is great. I'm looking forward to it. Work has been extremely boring without you here."

"Now I know you're lying. Work is never boring," I said. It felt good that she missed me even if she was the only one. I'd only spoken to Erin since coming here. I received a few random texts from people I considered friends who didn't even know I was gone. I was invited to two parties, a fundraiser, and was reminded of my upcoming dentist appointment.

"Nobody gets me like you do. Take care of yourself. I'll call you in a few days." Erin disconnected the call before I could even say good-bye.

I pulled up my article on my laptop. The fishing story was informative and fun, and it had great photos. The sanctuary story was brilliant. My heart was woven throughout the feature in the language and accompanying photos. I knew Erin would be pleased. I closed it and opened my journal. A lot of it was about the sanctuary, but most of it was about Brynn. I was emotional and had written my thoughts with care and love.

Love? I barely stopped myself from panicking. I could love an idea, or a place, or a group of people and animals, right? Love meant what was inside of me and having a positive connection with those around me. I loved Wally. I didn't think I would, but he was on my mind a lot. And the work at the sanctuary—Tina, Rick, Roger, Brody. All of the hurt animals made my soul bleed, but knowing they would make it out in the wild or even a life at the beautiful sanctuary made the journey and emotional investment so worth it.

And Brynn. She was wonderful. I didn't love her. I was incapable of romantic love, right? My heart had been tucked away for so long that it seemed so unlikely that it would make an appearance now. I mean, I was leaving in a few days. It needed to stay safely inside. I paced the room to help me expel energy. Was I in love with Brynn? We'd known each other three weeks. Less than a month. Nobody fell in love that quickly. I was just grateful for her in my life and the thousands of times she saved me. Love wasn't when my heart fluttered when I saw her, or how my breath hitched when she walked over to me. She was beautiful and strong, but that was only physical appreciation. I thought about her all of the time, but I was in her house and in her bed. That was geographical. Love was something different. Love was wanting to be around a person and accepting their flaws and weaknesses. It was the need to touch, hold, please, console, support, and satisfy.

What I felt for Brynn was all of that. I sank down on the couch. I was in love with Brynn Coleman. She was my first thought of the day, and my last when I fell asleep in her arms at night. How did this happen? I started a new page and jotted down everything I felt. I didn't stop until Brynn and Wally came home.

"Are you okay?" Brynn dropped the bag of groceries on the counter and sank to her knees in front of me. "Did something happen? "There was such concern on her face. She touched my cheek lovingly. Did Brynn love me, too? Did we both slip?

"No, I'm fine." I put my hand on top of hers.

"You're white as a sheet. Have you eaten today?" she asked. That was a good question. I'd been writing for hours. We both knew how easy it was for me to forget about time when I was engrossed.

"Um, well. I don't know." I was honest.

She stood up. "Okay, I'm making an early dinner. I want you to relax for the next thirty minutes. That means no laptop, no cell phone, nothing. Your butt stays right there. Wally can keep you company if you want." She was so cute when she was serious. I watched her move around the kitchen, gracefully and quietly. Dinner was a chicken casserole. I couldn't remember the last time I had a casserole, but it smelled delicious.

"Tell me about your day," I said.

Before cooking, Brynn had untucked her uniform shirt, loosened her tie, and rolled up her sleeves. I loved watching the nightly ritual. Her hair looked perfect, and messy, and I wanted to touch her. I was desperate to feel her, to run my hands through her hair, to feel her against me.

"Do I have to stay right here? I missed you today." I pointed to the couch, my prison, and she crooked her finger at me. I quickly jumped up and walked over to her.

"I thought about you all afternoon, but I didn't want to bother you because I knew you were busy getting your story done. Are you finished?" She put her arms around my waist and pulled me closer. I leaned into her and sighed. She smelled fresh and outdoorsy.

"I'm getting there. I talked to my boss who asked when she was going to see something. I promised her everything by tomorrow. I'm basically finished. Just one last read through and a few minor changes." She kissed the top of my head and we stood there like that until Wally decided he wanted in on the cuddle action. Brynn reached for him.

"Come here, big guy. Did you tell Kennedy how you wowed the crowd today? How you were super sweet and had your picture taken a zillion times?" She flipped him and I rubbed his belly until he started nipping at my fingers playfully.

"I bet you're an internet star and you don't even know it." I made a mental note to check YouTube later. "How big is he going to be? Or will he just stay this size?"

Brynn laughed. "Oh, no. He could get up to fifty pounds. I'm hoping he was the runt of the litter and only gets to be about thirty pounds."

"That's huge. I had no idea. I wish he would stay this size forever. He's so adorable." I rubbed both of his ears. Wally closed his eyes in contentment.

"Let's take this giant baby over to the couch. Dinner will be ready in about twenty minutes. Do you need something to nibble on in the meantime?" She was always so thoughtful.

"I'm fine. I can wait that long." I skipped a lot of meals back home. This wasn't unusual.

Wally scurried off to find his tennis ball and Brynn pulled me back to lean against her. She took the ball from Wally's mouth and tossed it behind the couch. He panted and scurried off to fetch it.

"He's so much like a dog," I said. Having never had a dog before, I was going by what I read in books and saw on television.

"He will sleep hard when he finally relaxes. Most days he gets a great nap in, but today was busy at the sanctuary." She threw the ball for him over and over until the timer went off for dinner.

I sighed and moved out of the way. I missed the warmth and weight of her arm across my chest as she held me. We washed up and prepared our plates. Dinner smelled delicious. It was comfort food and I smiled during the entire meal. Brynn's life was far more interesting than mine and she answered every question I asked. What was her favorite television show? When did she have her first kiss? What did she do for fun around Anchorage?

After feeding Wally, we retired to the couch where she resumed holding me. I talked about ten times more than she did. When she fell asleep, I left the comfort of her embrace. I finished editing the article, separated all of the photos I wanted to send, and finished my journal with tonight's entry of the sweet exchange Brynn and I had. I only had a few days left here. I blocked out leaving from my head and my heart. I didn't want to think about the heartache I would feel after leaving this place. Who knew that I, Kennedy Wells, self-absorbed, self-assured southern California snob, was capable of being heartbroken?

❖

"I'm so sorry I fell asleep last night. You should've woken me." Brynn voice was gravelly in my ear. I moaned as she ran her hands up and down my back apologetically.

I didn't tell her that I tried on several occasions, but she refused to wake up. "I've kept you up late several nights in a row. You needed your sleep." She drew circles and random designs on my skin. My body broke out in chill bumps. "That feels good. And after about thirty more minutes of this, I'll accept your apology." She poked me playfully and made me giggle. I rested my chin on her shoulder. I wanted to see her. "Thank you for everything, Brynn. For helping me out and always being there for me. I couldn't have done any of this without you. I would've given up on Alaska weeks ago."

She gave me a quick you're welcome squeeze and twirled my hair around her fingers. "Did you get everything done?"

"Yes. I was pretty tired, but I emailed the files and photos to Erin right before I dragged you off the couch," I said.

"So, you're finished."

I nodded. "I told her I would wait until I heard back from her before I made plans to go home. There might be some photo she wants or an interview I need to do. And I'm not using any of the company's money since I'm here with you." We lay there quietly. I was dying to know what was on her mind. I was so confused and nervous.

She had made it very clear that she wasn't the kind of person who jumped in without thinking. She kept her distance from women like me. The noncommittal kind. Funny how nothing else mattered to me but moments with Brynn. My articles were stellar. Erin and Travis were going to love them. I should have been happy. I just didn't want to go home. I kissed Brynn's shoulder.

"We should probably get up, huh? Can I go with you today?" Her lips curved in her crooked smile. "I would love that. Today we're going to drive around and check the lots again. It's boring so having you as company will make my day." She brushed a kiss on my forehead. Playtime was over and we needed to get our day started. "Meet me in the shower?" She slipped out from beneath me and padded into the bathroom, naked, confident, and beautiful.

I was going to miss her. The way she moved, the way she smelled, the way she protected me. I was going to miss Wally, this cabin, the town, my new friends, the food, and the thrill of the outdoors. I brushed an errant tear away. I was even going to miss Martha, the moose that destroyed my rental car. Well, maybe not her, but being up close and personal with nature. I allowed myself thirty more seconds of wallowing, then joined Brynn in the shower.

*B*REAKTHROUGH

Chapter Twenty-four

The cabin of the Jeep felt small. I was unbelievably sad at the thought of leaving this life at the drop of a phone call from my boss. Brynn seemed lost in her thoughts, too. I wanted to know what she was thinking, but I was afraid her thoughts didn't mirror mine and that terrified me. I'd rather go home with my chin up and my heart breaking, than admit I was in love and skulk away with the carcass of what was left of my heart dragging behind me. I couldn't bear the thought of Brynn not feeling anything for me. She liked me, liked my company, but was there anything more? How did the rest of the world act in a situation like this? I was at a loss. I needed to turn to a friend for advice. Erin was the first person to pop into my head but I knew she wasn't going to encourage me to follow my heart. No, she would want me to follow the next story. She wasn't heartless, but she was a businesswoman.

"I could use another cup of coffee," I said.

"I'm sorry I fell asleep early." Brynn reached over and squeezed my hand. I missed her warmth when she let go. "How long will it take your boss to read your article?"

I shrugged. "She'll put it at the top of her list since it's the feature and she wants her little brother to succeed. I'm sure after Travis meets with the production team and shows them everything, he or Erin will let me know what they need. She might be okay with it all."

• 185 •

"So you could leave as soon as tomorrow." Her voice was void of emotion.

"Well, I could take a day or two of personal time, if we wanted to spend more time together." I couldn't look at her. I pretended to find something really interesting outside my window. I wanted her to beg me to take that time. I wanted her to pull the Jeep over, hold me in her arms, kiss me soundly, and tell me that was the best idea she'd ever heard.

"I would like that. Maybe I could take a few days, too, and I can show you more of Alaska," she said. I smiled. She wanted to spend more time with me, too. "There's a great half-day trip over to Kodiak Island where we can watch bears up close and personal. Or we could go kayaking."

"You want me in the water? That cold Alaskan water? Are you kidding me? Baby steps, Brynn. Baby steps," I said.

"Okay, maybe we'll do the bear trip instead."

"Or we could just stay at the cabin."

She raised her eyebrow at me. "I do owe you a really good night."

"You don't owe me anything. You've done everything for me. Professionally and personally, and I've enjoyed every single minute with you." I caressed her arm. I loved the way her muscles twitched under my touch.

"Entirely my pleasure. And I mean that." She sounded sexy and confident, like she did two nights ago when she flipped me over and did things to me that nobody had ever done before.

"I'm going to miss you and your confidence." I ruined the moment with my confession. The smile slid off of her face. She gave a curt nod and turned back to face the road. Fuck. My timing sucked. I was so bad at this relationship stuff. It was just easier to slip out at night. "So, anything from Lara?" Not that I wanted to talk about the investigation, but it was safer than chatting about our emotions.

"Nothing new. She said the Department of Fish and Game hadn't received any reports of anything out of the ordinary, but they are on alert," she said.

"What does that mean?"

"Hunters have to report their big game or if they've witnessed anything out of the ordinary. For every bad hunter out there, there are ten good ones who do things by the book," she explained.

"I was hoping we'd get this resolved before—" Again, I said the wrong thing. "I mean, I hope they catch them soon."

"Me, too. But if it happens when you are back in California, I doubt they would need you for anything. Most of these don't go to trial. Especially when there is an eye witness. It usually gets handled between the lawyers." Brynn pulled into the parking lot where a tiny coffee shack sat. It was more of a kiosk and it smelled wonderful. "What do you want?"

"Bold, two creamers, two sugars." My eyes throbbed this morning from lack of sleep and the brightness of the sun. It radiated off of everything. I wanted a dreary day that matched my mood. I checked my emails even though it was too early for Erin. Nothing other than every single store offering some type of great sale. The only thing I was excited to get back to in California was my wardrobe. Even though I loved the new jeans I bought for the trip, I wanted to throw them away because I had worn them so many times over the past several weeks.

"What are you looking forward to the most when you get home?" Brynn asked. It was like she read my mind.

"All of my clothes. I swear I was just thinking that. I mean, these clothes are fine and the boots are comfortable, but I miss dressing up and feeling pretty. Sounds stupid, huh?" She reached over to cup my chin and lifted it so my gaze met hers.

"You are beautiful wearing anything and nothing at all. I love seeing you in my flannel shirts and even my boxers to bed. I'm sure you are a knockout all dressed up on the red carpet, but I think you are gorgeous sitting here, right next to me."

I almost swooned at her sincerity. "Oh, stop it. You're just trying to make me feel good." I leaned over and kissed her cheek. "It's working," I whispered. I felt her smile against my lips.

Brynn checked the maps in the marquee at the first trailhead to ensure they were well stocked and poked around the garbage and recycle receptacles. She talked to a couple who just arrived and gave them her business card. I was sure it was to caution them about the poachers and to be careful in general. We did that all morning and well into the afternoon. It wasn't glamorous, but we got to spend time together.

I was the one who answered questions this time around. Why I was scared of animals, what I was allergic to, and who was my favorite band growing up. She wanted to know my first word, the last time I stayed up all night, and if I liked fireworks. Her questions were so random and charming.

"Do you feel like going out for dinner tonight?" Brynn asked after we finished our rounds.

"Honestly? Only if it's quick. I'd like to spend some quiet time alone with you, if that's all right." The clock was ticking on our time together.

"We can do a drive by at Lucille's. Does anything sound good? I can call it in." We decided on the fried chicken special. While I transferred our stuff to the truck, Brynn grabbed Wally and called in our order. Wally crawled to my lap and we headed into town to get a quick dinner.

I was nervous that I hadn't heard from Erin yet. I knew that she, or her assistant, opened my email because I had the read receipt in my inbox. I learned that trick a long time ago, especially when dealing with deadlines. That tiny feature saved me a time or two.

Brynn put the food in her storage locker in the bed of the truck. The smells would've been too much of a distraction for Wally and both of us would've had to hold him back from digging into it the entire drive home. He was well behaved, but still an animal.

When we were only a few minutes away from the cabin, Brynn said, "We can watch a movie this evening if you want."

"I'd like to take a walk with you," I said. Brynn's property was so lovely and I wanted to see it when we weren't so stressed. "Can Wally come with us or no?"

"A walk sounds nice, but it's not the best idea to bring him with us. We would spend our walk corralling him, pulling him off of trees, chasing him away from holes in the hills. Taking Wally for a walk is more of a workout." I vividly pictured Brynn doing all of those things with Wally and laughed at the visual.

"You paint a hilarious picture. Yeah, okay, we'll leave him home." Home. I slipped into this role so quickly. Brynn's girlfriend. Wally's surrogate. It was a nice fantasy.

CHAPTER TWENTY-FIVE

I liked the feel of Brynn's hand in mine. Her fingers were long and soft, and I remembered them touching my body over and over. She gave my hand a tug and pulled me close for a kiss. It was tender and maybe I was reading too much into it, but I felt her heart in that kiss. I had no reason to tell her anything, no reason to give either of us hope, but I needed to say something.

"I'm sorry," I said. She nodded at me. She lifted her fingertips to glide over my cheeks, touching my face everywhere as if to memorize me. I closed my eyes and leaned into her hands.

"It's okay." She wiped away the first few tears that fell. She kissed away the rest. "It's okay." She repeated that over and over until I fell against her and gave in to my tears. She held me tightly and stroked my hair until I stopped crying.

I sniffled and pulled back from her soaked shirt. "I'm sorry I'm so emotional. I don't know what's going on with me," I said.

She brushed away the last of my tears with her fingertips. "It's hard. I'm just trying not to think about it. Wally and I got used to you being around. Thank you for staying with us. I know it was because of bad circumstances, but it's been a nice time with you."

My lip quivered as I tried not to cry again. "Thank you for taking care of me. You were always at the right place at the right time. What treats do moose eat?"

She looked confused. "Usually leaves, water lilies, stuff like that. Why?"

"I feel like I should leave something special for Martha and Tuffy. It's because of them that we're together." I shook my head at that memory. It seemed like a lifetime ago. She laughed at my joke. God, I was going to miss that sound. "She's like the sheep. She spent a few weeks at Spa Sanctuary and has a hard time leaving," Brynn said. "Can we go back home? I think I'm done crying." She kissed my hand several times while we walked back to the cabin. "This place is so beautiful, Brynn. I get why you live here."

In my head, I was pointing out all the differences between our two homes. I loved the craziness of Los Angeles in a weird, twisted way. Being away from it so long, though, I found that I really didn't miss it. I rarely slept, my eating habits were terrible, and I didn't make a bit of difference to anybody. My friends were all work related. They were pleasant enough, but I couldn't remember ever going over to someone's house just to have a nice dinner and chat. There was always a catch. A meaning behind all of our actions. Here in Alaska, I started from scratch. There were people here who genuinely liked me. They didn't want something from me, or expect anything in return other than friendship.

"What are you thinking about?" Brynn put her arm around my shoulders while we walked.

"I was thinking about myself. Sounds selfish, right? I feel like I've made some kind of breakthrough here in Alaska. I don't feel like I'm the same person I was when I got here. Does that make sense?"

"It completely makes sense. Alaska has a way of stripping a person down and showing her what's really important in this world. You can't be this close to nature and not understand its significance," she said.

"I'm just surprised at how much it's affected me. And not just because we happened. People here are friendly—"

"Except for the poachers chasing you," Brynn interrupted. Her arm tightened possessively.

I smiled. "Except for the poachers. It's small town life in a bigger city. Anchorage is good-sized. Honestly, when I came here, I was expecting something less civilized. I mean, I knew there were hotels and fast food restaurants. But there is still so much local flavor and culture mixed in."

"That's why I love this place so much. I can run into town to catch a concert or movie, or I can take a walk on a trail ten minutes from town and not see a single person," Brynn said. She opened the door for me when we got back to the cabin. Wally greeted us with whimpers and hugs.

"He's so attached to you," I said.

Brynn scooped him up and tossed him on the couch. They wrestled around for a bit while I jumped in the shower and got ready for bed. I wasn't tired, so I started a mystery book on my kindle.

"Sorry it took so long. He was rather rambunctious, but I got him to expel a lot of energy," she said. She stripped to her sports bra and boxers and turned on the shower. She peeked her head back around the corner and winked at me. "I'll be back in a flash."

My heart raced as visions of what she was going to do to me filled my head. I looked at the oversized T-shirt and boxers and decided it wasn't sexy enough. I jumped out of bed, traded the boxers for my black panties, and found a white tank top in Brynn's dresser. I was sure she wouldn't mind. I piled my hair high and surveyed myself in the mirror. I still had it. When Brynn turned off the shower, I suppressed a squeal and jumped back into bed. She walked out of the bathroom wearing only a towel.

"You win." I leaned up on my knees and reached out to her.

"Nice tank." She rubbed her thumbs across my hard nipples and I shuddered.

"Nice towel," I said and slowly removed it. Fuck, I loved her body. Standing in front of me, naked, muscular, and sexy, she was everything I wanted in a woman. Strong, determined, and not ashamed to give or seek pleasure. I touched her stomach and watched chills explode across her body. "You're still wet."

"Oh, you have no idea how much." She leaned forward and pushed me back onto the mattress. I smiled at her. I didn't want to think about tomorrow or the future. I just wanted to enjoy us right here, right now. "I want to make this a night neither one of us forgets."

I traced her face. I loved touching her. "I could never forget you, Brynn." I pulled her head to me and placed a gentle, meaningful kiss on her lips. It started off soft, but the second she started rolling her hips into me, I deepened it. Her tongue teased mine, touching it softly, licking the sides. I sucked it into my mouth. I needed her to consume me. She moaned into my mouth. Her body stiffened with the need to release. She broke our kiss and reached down to lift my legs onto her shoulders.

"I need these off." She pulled at my panties.

I was only able to free one leg from them before she spread her hands on my hips and pulled me into her. My panties were forgotten when I felt her wet pussy against mine. We both moaned at the intimate contact. She pushed against me and we found a fantastic rhythm. She slid my legs back down onto the bed and I splayed them shamelessly for her. Every part of me was hers. She made me feel adored. I closed my eyes when I felt her hands run up and down my thighs, possessively, eagerly. I bucked into her hand when she massaged my slit.

"I'm yours," I said. I felt her hesitation at my confession for only a fraction of a second.

She slid two fingers inside of me and I lifted my hips to get her deeper inside me. I opened my eyes and watched as she fucked me. I wanted to go slow and savor the moment, but we had all night so I greeted my first orgasm with a sharp cry. The second, only moments later, was just as intense. I shook so badly that she stopped to give me a break. She stretched out beside me and kissed my neck.

"You are mine," she said.

I put my hand on her chest. "Always." I meant it.

Brynn would always have a piece of my heart whether we were together or thirty-five hundred miles apart. She managed to get me to do something I hadn't done since my first love. She made me fall again. She made me realize that I wasn't lost, I only needed to be found. She was there for me at every turn. Brynn was too good for me. I didn't deserve her, but I sure as hell was going to make this night one we both remembered for a long time. I leaned up, kissed her, and pushed her back so I was on top. Brynn was not one to wait for anything. She pressed her hands into mine and ran them over her breasts, down her stomach, and rested them on my thighs.

"I need to feel you inside of me," she said.

I slipped my hand between us to rub her slick, swollen mound. My movements were restricted since I was straddling her, but I found it highly erotic watching Brynn become even more aroused. When she pressed her hips up into me, I pushed down to give her the tight friction she wanted.

"You're killing me." She groaned. She clenched my hips and bucked against my hand. I was stunned when she came after only a few seconds of movement. I ran my hands over her body while she relaxed.

"That was amazing." I had never seen anybody come that way. I was empowered by the whole experience, but slightly disappointed. I wanted Brynn to come in my mouth; her hand on my head, her pussy grinding against me. It was still beautiful to watch her orgasm even if it wasn't the way I pictured.

"That surprised me, too," she said. I leaned forward and kissed her. "I haven't come like that in a long time."

"You are incredible. And sensitive." I cuddled on top of her and smiled as she ran her fingertips up and down my back. I brushed her damp hair out of her face. "You have the prettiest eyes. Sometimes they are gray, sometimes they are almost black. I can always tell when you are upset or turned on just by their color."

"Oh, yeah? What color are they now?" Brynn asked.

"It's dark in here, so I can't tell, but I'm going to guess they're dark."

"The first day I saw you, I noticed your eyes. You have tiny copper color flecks in your big brown eyes. I even told you that. It's so unique." She kissed me. "That's how you get all the girls, isn't it? Damsel in distress, big, flirty eyes." I poked her side. She giggled and grabbed my fingers. "I've got a better place for these."

"Should I guess where?" I loved when she was playful.

"I'll narrow it down. Somewhere on my body, but not my sides." I traced a path with my fingertip over her collarbone, across one breast, over to the other.

"Here?"

"That's nice, but not what I had in mind." She smiled crookedly at me.

I raised an eyebrow at her. I leaned on my side and continued my trek down her body. I stopped at her belly button. "Here?" I circled a pattern around it until she giggled.

"Also not what I had in mind."

I purposely skipped her pelvic area and moved to her legs. I stopped at her knee. "What about here?"

She sighed heavily. "Nope. You went too far." She picked up a strand of my hair that fell across her chest and twirled it gently around her fingers. "I thought you knew me better than that." Challenge accepted.

"Oh. Maybe you mean here?" I trailed my hand to the juncture of her thighs. She pressed her hand against mine and stopped it from moving away.

"This, right here, is a good start." She closed her eyes and continued playing with my hair while I touched the velvety folds of my favorite place on her body. She relaxed and tensed under my stroking.

When I pressed harder, she gasped. She was ready to come again. I lowered my head and followed the same trail as my fingers. She grabbed my hair and held it while I spread her apart and tasted her. The tangy sweetness of her filled my mouth as I sucked on her swollen clit. In the short time we were together, I'd learned exactly what to do to maximize her pleasure. I edged her a few times before giving her another orgasm. I loved hearing her deep moans and wanted to memorize her sounds. When she came, she was loud and held me close until she was finished.

I rested my head on her thigh and waited until her body slowed. "This is a nice place to be."

We were both sluggish in the afterglow of our love making. It was definitely love but I didn't want to ruin our close moment by blurting it out so I, for once, kept quiet and enjoyed the solitude of us.

CHAPTER TWENTY-SIX

Erin wants to have a conference call at ten." I looked at Brynn and saw a flicker of panic before she masked it with a nod.

"Okay, that's good news, right?" She slid her belt around her waist and fastened it on the fifth hole. She sat on the bed to finish tying her shiny, black boots. She paused to buff out a smudge with the pad of her thumb.

"I love you in your uniform," I said. She froze. I froze. Even though it was said in a different context, it was there between us. She didn't look at me. "It fits you so well." She stood and adjusted her tie before she turned.

"Thank you. I hate that I have to wear one, but at least it's comfortable." She pulled me into her arms. "So, I guess that means you'll have to stay here today, huh?"

I frowned. "Yes. That way I have access to everything if she has specific questions or concerns. I hope you don't mind."

She kissed the tip of my nose. "I understand. Wally and I will just have to make it without you. We will celebrate whatever news you get tonight with great food and maybe another nice walk."

"I would like that," I said. I made a mental note to stay away from the word 'love' until I was long gone from this place. "Have a good day, dear." It was a joke, but it felt good to say. Brynn tilted her ranger hat at me and she and Wally disappeared down the drive.

I grabbed my computer to read Erin's mail again. It was simple and just said she wanted to talk. I was on edge yesterday when I didn't hear from her. It was ten times worse today. Three hours. I had three hours to kill. My journal was up-to-date except for last night's entry.

I decided to see what was happening in Hollywood. It turned out that I didn't care about who had a baby, or who trashed a hotel room, or who got engaged. That news was all boring to me. I was upset when I got to Alaska because I felt like I was being punished. Now, I felt like Alaska had cleansed me. No wonder people had a hard time getting back into the swing of things after a long vacation. A vacation was a peek at another possibility. I looked at the time. Only an hour had passed.

What if they hated it? I thought I rocked it, but maybe Travis thought it was too emotional and not as informative as he expected it to be. Erin chose me for my celebrity interview skills. Maybe my reporting ability wasn't up to the standard they were looking for.

A walk was out of the question. If I missed Erin's call, she would not be happy. The cabin was spotless so I couldn't busy myself with housework. My laundry was caught up. There wasn't a single thing I could do to occupy my time except watch a show or a movie. I started a movie on my laptop that I had seen a dozen times and did my best to ignore the time and my phone. When the call came in, I jumped and answered it immediately.

"This is Kennedy." Force of habit, even though I knew it was Erin.

"So we read everything you sent."

"What did you think of the articles?" I asked.

"Oh, the articles were great. Fantastic even. Travis has a few suggestions, but they can be handled when you're back in California."

"Oh, that's such a relief." I relaxed for the first time all morning.

"But that's not what I called about."

"Okay." I was missing something. "Why did you call?"

"I think the real gem is your journal."

I was completely confused. "What are you talking about?"

"Your diary or journal or whatever you want to call it. I read that all day. I couldn't put it down. All of the issues you've had there. It was fantastic. The best I've ever read from you. I think you should write a book." Whatever she was talking about, she was dead serious.

"Wait a minute. How did you get my journal?" Did I send it to her by mistake? I pulled up my sent files.

"It was in your Dropbox. I just assumed you wanted me to read it," she said.

I wanted to die, I was so embarrassed. My boss read my most intimate details, my thoughts, my feelings about Brynn, our sex life, the poaching, the sanctuary. That journal documented every single thing I did in Alaska. "I didn't mean for you to read it. The sanctuary and the fishing articles were the only thing that should've been shared."

"Kennedy, relax. I thought you meant for me to read it. I never would have read it otherwise. You should know it is a beautiful story. You should absolutely turn it into a book. I know that's asking a lot, but if you agree to this, you can have anything you want." Erin wasn't kidding.

"I just can't believe you read all the things I put in that journal."

"Please. It's not like we have many secrets," Erin said.

"Yeah, I guess you're right." Nikki Toles, a girl I hadn't thought about for weeks, popped in my head. I snorted. She was a lifetime ago.

"The feature is perfect. People are going to read it and appreciate what is being done there. They will donate. I've seen it happen before. It's your best work. So heartfelt. And people love saving animals," she said.

"Except for the poachers," I said.

"You really care, don't you?" Erin didn't give me time to answer. "Of course you do. I already read how much you care. Here's something. Do you feel comfortable writing about poaching? Maybe just how it's a problem and the consequences? I think it would enhance the importance of the sanctuary and the rangers. I could give you a few more days there."

The wheels in my head started spinning. She was right. I already had enough information about illegal hunting. I lived it for the past week. And it was something concrete I could do to help. "I could do that." Plus, I would get more time with Brynn.

"I'm also serious about you writing a book about how a city girl survives the great outdoors. You could make it a self-help book or turn your journal into a memoir and expand more. I can't tell you how many times I laughed out loud."

I calmed down quickly at the realization of me not only hitting a home run, but a grand slam with this entire Alaskan experience. I couldn't stop smiling. "So, a book, huh?"

"Yes, but let's get everything done for *Antlers & Anglers* first."

"You said Travis liked the articles?" He was a kid, but he was also one of my bosses so I needed his approval.

"Oh, he was excited, especially about all of the photos. You're right. We're going to have a hard time narrowing down the pictures. He even talked about adding a few pages of just photos."

"Okay, give me a few days and I'll get you the poaching bit." I already had the ever important lead paragraph written in my head.

"Thanks. Hey, Kennedy? Great job," she said.

I hung up and did a happy dance all around Brynn's cabin. I wanted to celebrate and I wanted it to be with Brynn. I grabbed the car keys. I couldn't cook, but I knew how to bake and nobody said no to my German chocolate cake. I shot Brynn a text message to let her know where I was going and carefully headed to the grocery store. I was wary of animals and humans. As I drove into town, I waved at people I didn't know who waved at me first. When I saw Mandy walking to Lucille's, I slowed to make sure she saw my wave. She stopped in the crosswalk and motioned me over. I rolled down the window.

"Hey. How are you? How are the articles coming?" Her smile and demeanor were so genuine I kind of melted a little. My new friends were awesome.

"Better than I expected. I just heard from my boss. It's good news. I'm baking a cake to celebrate. Do you and Lisa want to come over for dessert later?" I was holding up traffic, but nobody seemed to care.

"I'll check with her and call you later, okay?" I nodded. She tapped the car and continued on the crosswalk. I waved my hand out of the window to apologize for delaying the cars behind me. Several of them nodded in understanding.

I pulled into the parking lot of the grocery store and pulled up the recipe on my phone. I had no idea what Brynn had in her pantry so I started from scratch. My cart was full by the time I checked out. Still no message from Brynn. She must have been in a dead zone. I spent the drive back thinking about the poaching article and wondering if I should make it personal, too, or just a general informative piece about poaching.

I parked Brynn's car where I found it and lugged the groceries inside. Baking a cake from scratch took about three hours. I planned on having it done by the time she got home. I sat on the couch for a moment to read through the instructions.

My email chimed as my laptop connected to the slow Wi-Fi. I pulled it up and saw an email from Travis about the photographs I sent in. He marked the photos he was going to use. I was ecstatic the photo of Brynn and the elk made the pile. Other winners included Tina fixing the puffin's wing, the rangers wrestling with the elk, the impressive entrance to the sanctuary where Melissa and Yogi were grazing close-by. Alaska, in all of her wilderness, was beautiful. Travis ended the email with praise about the articles I'd already sent. I had to be careful or Travis was going to ask me to come over to *A&A* permanently.

I was momentarily sidetracked by a shadow that drifted across the kitchen wall. When I looked up, I saw a person peeking in the kitchen window. Thank God the groceries were piled high enough on the counter to hide my body. I slid to the ground and waited.

"I know she's inside. I followed her here after I called you all." It was a whisper, but because Brynn's place was so quiet, I could hear every word.

Fuck. The poachers found me. How the fuck did they find me? They had to have seen me at the grocery store or talking to Mandy. I reached my phone and realized it was on the counter. They would see me for sure if I grabbed it. The handle on the front door jiggled slightly. I had to make a decision. I crept to the counter and reached for my phone.

"I see her." His shadow made circling motions. He was probably telling the others to surround the place.

I grabbed my phone and headed down the hall. I dialed Brynn's number with shaky fingers. When she didn't answer, I was at a loss at who to call. The second I heard glass breaking, I dialed 9-1-1, ran into the mudroom, and locked the door. The window on the door was too small for anyone to climb through, and the door was thick lumber. It would take them some time to break through that. When Brynn was giving me a tour, she told me about a crawl space under the house. There was a small trapdoor in the floor. That had to be where it led. It was my only option. The operator finally picked up.

"Hello?" I whispered so the poachers wouldn't immediately know where I was in the house. Brynn kept all the doors closed because of Wally. "I need you to patch me through to Trooper Lara Ridgley right now."

"What's your emergency?" I felt like I had the same operator as the day Martha destroyed my car. Was my luck that bad?

"This is Kennedy Wells. I witnessed a group of poachers last week. Trooper Lara Ridgley said they were dangerous. They just found where I've been hiding. Please patch me through or let her know right now." I swore if I ever met this person I would wring his neck.

"I'll get her on the line."

While I waited, I grabbed the handle to open the trapdoor and struggled to open it. It was heavy, especially since I was juggling a cell phone. They would get through the door eventually and I needed to not be in this room when they did.

"Kennedy, what's going on?"

I teared up when I heard Lara's voice. "They're here. At Brynn's. She's at work and they found me, Lara." I was squeezing the phone.

A voice came from outside the mudroom door. "Come on out. We just want to talk to you." I got chills at the sound of the poacher's voice. I knew if they caught me, I was a goner.

"I'm sending units. They'll be there in less than ten. Stay hidden."

"Thanks, Lara."

"Don't hang up. Keep the line open, okay?"

"I can't talk. And I need my hands," I said.

"Just put it in your pocket. We'll be there soon, Kennedy. Hang on."

I slipped my phone in my back pocket and finally levered the door open. It was heavy and dusty and before I had a chance to investigate the darkness below, there was a loud bang at the mudroom door. I jumped at the noise. A moment later, there was another bang and the hinges on the door bent as he threw his weight against it.

"She's in here."

I crawled into the space and closed the door behind me. It would be obvious where I had gone, but my plan was to find a hiding spot underneath the cabin and hope they thought I ran off. I scurried along the underbelly of the cabin, tearing my jeans on jagged rocks, scraping my palms on the dirt and tiny rocks. I had no idea where I was going.

I pulled out my phone and turned on the flashlight for a moment to get my bearings. The call was still live. I ignored the cobwebs and whatever the hell was clinging to them and focused on staying alive. There was a pile of stacked wood and a small wheelbarrow ten feet ahead. That was going to be my hiding place. I army crawled to the pile and hid behind it the best I could. I moved the wheelbarrow a bit to cover my legs.

My heart hammered and I had to hold my breath for fear they would hear my panting. I just needed to stay hidden for seven more minutes. That was it. There was a crash when they got through the mudroom door. Moments later, I heard the trap door open. I pressed flat against the dirt and prayed.

"She's either under the house or escaped. Take a look around." He yelled to one, two, three, a dozen men surrounding Brynn's cabin. I had no idea how many there were. I just knew I was not moving from this spot. If they found me, they would have to drag me out kicking and screaming.

Six more minutes. I saw a beam of light flash over my head, bounce on the back of the wall, and swirl around. He didn't see me. I heard him shut the door and walk across the cabin. His steps were heavy and hurried. I heard him murmur to others. Their feet shuffled overhead as they expanded their search for me.

Four minutes. I was almost in the clear. I heard the rumble of engines and tires crunching over gravel and my heart jumped, thinking Lara was finally here. I peeked out, but was crushed when I realized it was the poachers. They must have hidden their trucks and walked up to the cabin to surprise me. It worked. My leg was cramping and I very carefully and very quietly stretched it out, but it was exactly at the wrong angle.

One second. That's all it took. In slow motion, the stack of logs I brushed with my toe tumbled and scattered. The sound reverberated. I looked up to survey the damage and was greeted with the barrel of a gun.

"Hello, sweetheart." Fuck.

CHAPTER TWENTY-SEVEN

I scurried to the other side, but the sound of the gun hammer cocking made me freeze.

"Come on out. Enough of this. If you make me crawl under there, you're going to regret it."

My mother always said my mouth would get me into trouble one day. Today was that day. "How many people talk with guns? Let's see, umm, criminals. Guilty people," I said.

"You're only making it harder on yourself."

I thought about staying put, but I was afraid they would just kill me instead of wrestling me out from under the house. I purposely left my phone by the wheelbarrow. I didn't want them to know I called 9-1-1. They would find out soon enough. Hopefully in three minutes. I needed to stall until then. I took my time crawling out. When I felt somebody's hands on my ankles, I knew I was in serious trouble. They yanked me out and dragged me, my face scraping the ground. I felt my cheek swell up. When we were far enough away from the house, they stopped and tossed my feet down.

"You can stop manhandling me. You caught me, okay?" I said.

"So, you're the one who's caused us all sorts of problems, huh?" The guy who spoke was a nice looking older man. I assumed he was the leader. He was probably somebody's grandfather. The kind who bought his granddaughter a pony or taught his grandson how to hunt at age five. His clothes were expensive and his hands manicured and clean. That scared me. Somebody else did his dirty work. If he was letting me see his face, he wasn't planning on letting me live long enough to identify him. This ring was bigger than Brynn, Lara, or anybody thought. I counted seven men total. Three I recognized from our initial run-in.

The leader reached out to help me up. I spit on it. It was the first time I'd ever spit and I was pleased with the results. My few victories the last minutes of my life were going to be small, but meaningful. His response was to laugh. The sound was wicked. He pulled out a bandana and wiped his hand. "Take her to the truck." He nodded at the guy I remembered as Randy and one of his other thugs. They grabbed me and pulled me to my feet.

"Look at what you did to my jeans," I said. They were torn at the knee in two places. I could complain about my jeans for a long time. "I can't wear these again." I leaned over to pluck at the torn fabric.

Randy laughed. "You have bigger problems than that, lady. Maybe you don't realize the trouble you're in." He twisted my arm and pushed me in front of him.

I yelped and stumbled forward. I had two minutes. Maybe less. I purposely tripped over a good-sized rock in my path. I needed Lara and her backup. I hoped she brought the entire police force with her. They pushed me forward until we reached the front of the cabin where the leader and the rest of his posse were waiting, looking impatient.

"People know about you. They know what you've done. Everybody's looking for you," I said. A few of them laughed. I made eye contact with Jim. "Especially you, Jim." I twisted to look at Randy. "And you, Randy." They shuffled uncomfortably.

"Well, we're here and I don't see anybody else," the leader said. He held his hands and looked around casually. "Nobody cares. Just get in the truck. We need to have a chat."

"Just a chat? We can have that here." I was stalling.

"We're not going to hurt you. We just need to clear up a few things and help you forget a few things you might have seen." His smile was deranged.

I was so fucked. "Why don't I believe that? You're pretty good at shooting helpless animals and getting rid of the evidence. Killing a person carries a steeper sentence, in case you were wondering. I gave all my photos to the police. If you think I'm joking about them looking for you, stick around town. Let's see how long you last." I pointedly stared at the ones I recognized. My bravery was stupid. I started praying.

"You're standing in front of seven men. Lying to us isn't doing you any favors."

"I don't need to lie. Those idiots already have their faces plastered all over Anchorage's police station. And you know that truck and trailer you destroyed?" I smiled with more confidence than I had. "Someone missed a tag. It's just a matter of time before they find you."

The leader barked a laugh that truly frightened me. I'd gone too far. "Put her in the truck. Let's get out of here," he said.

The men dispersed to their different trucks. I dug my boots into the ground and refused to move. The big guy who was responsible for escorting me to the truck slapped me across the face and yanked me forward.

"It's just going to get worse for you," he said.

My whole face stung. I realized it was too late and I started to cry. This was it for me. I would end up coyote meat somewhere in the Alaskan wild, far from civilization. People might find my remains two hundred years from now. I hadn't gotten the chance to tell Brynn I loved her.

I was five steps from the truck when six trooper cars raced up the driveway and fanned out to block the poachers in. It all happened so fast. Their lights were flashing, but there was no sound other than tires skidding to a halt on the gravel. Chaos erupted. Officers were everywhere with their guns drawn. The poachers had no idea what to do. I pushed away from the big guy and ran back toward the cabin. I wasn't going to be somebody's hostage. That never ended well.

"Freeze! Nobody move!"

I kept running, knowing I wasn't in trouble with the cops, but I needed to get away from the bad guys. The leader saw me make a run for it and lunged for me. Even he knew a hostage was the only way out of this for him. I heard two gunshots. My calf exploded with fire and chills. I hit the gravel. Alaska fucking hated me, I thought right before I passed out.

CHAPTER TWENTY-EIGHT

S he's going to be fine, Brynn. The bullet just grazed the outside of her leg. It only required three stitches. She can walk right out of here when we're done with the paperwork." Lara and Brynn's voices carried from the hallway. Lara explained the entire ordeal to Brynn who was overly concerned.

"Brynn, I'm okay," I said. Brynn pushed past Lara to get into my room. She was visibly distraught and more pale than normal. Her body shook when she pulled me into her arms. "It's okay. I'm fine."

"I should've been there with you. This wouldn't have happened."

"Don't think like that. If you'd been there, we would both have gotten hurt. I'm just glad it's over with and they finally caught the guys," I said.

Lara had reported that the leader was the owner of one of the largest construction companies in Alaska. There were a total of eleven men involved, according to the men the troopers had arrested. Officers were already headed to pick up the remaining four for questioning. Lara said they were sure more would surface during the investigation, but everyone was thankful the head of this beast was cut off.

"Does your leg hurt? Can you walk? I want to take you home."

I jokingly offered to drive. Brynn didn't seem like she was in any position to be behind the wheel of a vehicle. She leaned down to kiss me and stopped.

"What happened to your face?" The room was dark so she carefully tilted my cheek toward the light coming in from the hallway. She was barely keeping herself under control.

"It's just a scratch. I'll put some ice on it and the bruising will be gone in about a week. My leg stings a bit, but they gave me drugs so right now I don't care. The doctor said the scarring will be minimal."

Brynn hugged me again. "Fucking assholes. I would've shot them all if I was there." I believed her. "When can we leave? Who's your doctor? Let's try to speed this process up." She walked out of the room, a woman on a mission.

I was fine relaxing in the dark room. I was tired. Today felt like it lasted a week. I still had so much to do. Fuck. I didn't put the ingredients for the cake into the refrigerator. I needed to work on the poaching article because of the tight deadline. I didn't even know what time it was, or if it was the same day. I just wanted to sleep.

❖

"Babe, we're home." I woke up to Brynn gently shaking me awake.

"What time is it?" She scooped me into her arms like I weighed nothing and carried me into the cabin. "What happened to the groceries?"

"I put them away."

"Where's Wally?" I missed him. I was so thankful he wasn't home with me today. Those jerks would've shot him out of pure maliciousness.

"Given today's events, I decided another sleepover at Tina's was best for him." She nudged open the bedroom door with her foot and carefully placed me on the bed. She was so gentle and I was so needy from the drugs, I started crying. "It's okay. It's okay. We don't have to worry about them."

"I'm not worried about them," I said.

"What's wrong? Did I hurt you?" she asked. I shook my head. "What is it? Are the drugs wearing off?"

"No, it's stupid. Never mind," I said.

"Please tell me."

"My phone's under the house," I said.

"Your phone's under the house," she repeated.

I nodded. "When I was hiding, I left it by the stack of wood so that they wouldn't see that I called the police. I hate to ask, but can you get it for me?"

She kissed me softly and brushed my tender cheek. I tried not to wince under her touch even though she was gentle. "Anything for you." She tucked me in and went around the cabin to ensure all the windows and doors were locked. She was gone only five minutes. "Exactly where you said it was." She handed me my phone and I smiled like a kid getting a present.

I grabbed her by her shirt and pulled her down to kiss her. "Thank you, lover." The drugs were making me say weird things and my mood swings were all over the place. I was never this playful, but I loved the smile on her lips after I said it.

"I'm going to shower, change into something more comfortable, and I'll get a fire started in here. Are you hungry?" she asked. I watched her untie her boots and loosen her tie. She looked at me. "Babe? Are you hungry?"

"I love you. I love watching you undress. So methodical. And yeah, now that you mention it, I am kind of hungry. I wanted to make you a cake today because of my good news. Wasn't that amazing about Erin?" I fell back against the pillow and looked at my phone. I had a zillion text messages, and missed calls, and did I really just tell Brynn that I loved her? I looked up and met her wide eyes. "Did I just say that out loud?"

"Look, I know it's the drugs talking. Forget the shower. I'm going to cook something for you. I imagine you haven't had anything to eat all day." She bolted from the room.

I shouldn't have said anything, but it just felt so right. Brynn would be back in a few minutes. She needed to digest what I told her, and I needed to figure out what I missed during my hospital stay. I sent Erin a quick text message that basically said we caught the bad guys and I got shot. A second later, my phone rang.

"Are you fucking kidding me?" Erin's voice was two octaves higher than normal. "What happened? Are you okay?"

"I'm high. And have a few stitches, but I'm good. We caught seven guys today. No, eleven." I sounded loopy. I needed to focus harder.

"Slow down. How did you catch them?"

"They followed me to the cabin. I hid under the house, but they found me. Right when they were going to kidnap me, the cops arrived and I got shot."

"Kennedy, you're not making sense. Who shot you?" Her voice had an edge to it that I'd never heard before.

"I don't even know. I don't know if it was friendly fire, or one of bad guys got a shot off. I'll ask Brynn. Maybe she knows." I opened my laptop while she ranted about my misfortune. "So when do you want this article? I have an excellent ending for it." I laughed. She didn't.

"Okay, you are not allowed to work on this until you are healed and not on medication," she said sternly.

"I'm fine. Well, I will be in the morning. Tonight probably isn't the night to review your notes." I was too tired anyway.

"Don't worry about the article. You let that hot woman of yours take care of you. Call me when you feel better? And please, please take care of yourself." We hung up right when Brynn walked in with a tray of scrambled eggs, toast, and a large glass of orange juice.

"I hope you're joining me," I said. I made room for her.

"Well, only if you're in the mood for company." She seemed shy and nervous. "Let me grab a plate and a fork." She sat closer to me in the bed when she returned.

"I'm sorry I'm such a mess. I want to shower but I think I just need to eat and sleep," I said.

"Stop it. You're beautiful even scratched up and swollen."
She studied my face, but it looked like it pained her.

"It's bad, huh? I saw myself in the mirror before we left." I
patted my hair and scooped it back in a ponytail. I wanted to look
nice for Brynn, but I was tired and hungry.

"You look fine." She reached back and gave my foot a squeeze.
"I'm really sorry I didn't get your call. We were in a dead zone in a
valley." She was getting upset again. I touched her forearm.

"It's okay. I called Lara and she had the means to get to me
quickly. Everything turned out fine. They caught the bad guys so
we don't have to constantly look over our shoulders. I can go out
for a walk and not worry about getting kidnapped," I said.

Her chin quivered. "But I was supposed to take care of you.
I promised you I would." She looked down and curled the blanket
in her fist. "I begged you to stay here so that you would be safe."

"And I was. I screwed up by going out and not paying
attention to my surroundings. I'm sure one of the guys saw me at
the grocery store or in the parking lot. I got careless, not you."

"Eat what you can, then I want you to rest. We can talk in the
morning."

I nodded. I was almost too tired to eat, but I had enough spurts
of adrenaline to take a few bites of eggs and toast and finish my
orange juice. Brynn took the tray from me and knelt on the floor to
put her face close to mine. "I'm glad you are okay. I was worried
about you." She kissed my lips and wished me a good night.

"Are you not going to sleep with me?"

"I don't want to hurt you." She looked so sad.

"I want you to hold me tonight. It was a long day. Please?"

CHAPTER TWENTY-NINE

I blinked several times before my eyes finally focused. It was still early, but a look at the clock told me I had been asleep for ten hours. Brynn was still asleep. She was so afraid she would accidentally kick me while we slept, she had slept on top of the covers and as far away from my side as possible.

My leg throbbed, but I was able to walk. The bullet had shaved off a thin layer of muscle. A shower would be hard but no way was I going back to bed this dirty. A film of dust covered my skin and I was itching to clean up. I hobbled into the kitchen, found some cling wrap, and dressed my wound like a leftover. I would clean it and put a new bandage on after my shower.

I turned on the water, grabbed my shampoo and conditioner, and tackled my dirty body with vigor. The gravel damage was made obvious by the painful sting of soapsuds. My knees, my hands, my elbows, and my face all had battle wounds. Fucking assholes, I thought. My shower took twenty minutes. I didn't even try to shave. It just felt good to be clean. I sat on a bench in the bathroom and cleaned my calf the best I could. I was sure Brynn would help me the next time. I bandaged it and slipped on a pair of sweats and a T-shirt. It took forever to get a brush through my hair, but I didn't care. I was alive and finally clean.

"I would've helped you." Brynn's voice on the other side of the door made me yelp and drop my brush in fright. I stopped myself from cursing at her, though. That was a big step.

"Why do I get the feeling you are on the other side of the door smiling?" I opened it, but I was wrong. She stood there, tall, barely awake, not smiling. Her eyebrows furrowed with concern and her lips pinched together so tightly, they were white against her already pale skin. I touched her face lightly.

"I'm good. I even got my wound cleaned and dressed."

"Do you need your meds?" She stepped out of my way as I walked back to the bed. I tried not to limp for her sake.

"Absolutely not. If you have any ibuprofen, that would be great. The pain isn't severe." I stared at the bed. There were tiny clumps of dust and dirt all over the place. I looked at Brynn. "I did this? Can you help me change the sheets? I'm too clean to get back into this campsite. All that's missing is a bag of marshmallows."

She smiled weakly at my attempt at a joke. "Have a seat on the chair and I'll change the sheets." She grabbed a clean set from the linen closet and changed the bed in record time. We were going to have to talk about everything that happened yesterday, especially the part where I told her I loved her. For about two seconds in my drug induced haze, I was scared. Not anymore. I was at peace with my confession. I hope she was, too. "Would you like a fire in here?"

"That sounds great, but I know you have to work today and I can't be responsible for a fire. We already know I'm severely challenged by Earth's elements."

"Oh, I'm not leaving you alone today. Or tomorrow. I have the next forty-eight hours off unless there's an emergency. I'm yours to boss around," she said.

I frowned. Was I really bossy to Brynn? "I'm sorry if I haven't treated you well. I know I'm a princess and I know I'm difficult. You are such an amazing woman. If I made you feel less than perfect, I'm sorry."

"Stop talking. Crawl into bed. I'm going to shower and then we're going to talk about yesterday. All of it."

I liked it when she was playfully bossy with me. I saluted her and crawled under the covers. "I'm waiting."

She shook her head at me and closed the bathroom door. After a minute of waiting, I got bored. I was tired of being in the bedroom. I wanted sunlight and a cup of coffee. I threw off the covers and padded into the living room. I missed the brightness and happiness of this room. I made a quick cup of coffee and was sitting on the couch drinking it by the time Brynn was done with her shower.

"I was hoping you didn't get kidnapped again," she said.

I smiled, happy she could finally joke about it. "As much as I love the bedroom, I missed the beauty of this room. Plus, I wanted to watch you make me breakfast."

She leaned down and placed a soft and serious kiss on my lips. "You didn't eat much last night. How's your appetite?"

"I'm starving. Are you hungry?"

"Definitely. How about French toast?" she asked.

"Sounds yummy. Now, do you want to hear my good news?" I asked. If I remembered correctly, I still hadn't shared my conversation with Erin, though I dropped bits and pieces last night.

"I want you to tell me every second about your day yesterday. Leave nothing out." I smiled at her. She looked fierce standing in the kitchen, her gray eyes blazing. Her plaid long-sleeved shirt was tight and showed off her curves. I couldn't figure out why she was wearing jeans and looked like she was headed out.

"Why are you dressed?" I pouted because just ten minutes ago she said she was mine for two days.

"I thought you might want me to pick up Wally so he can be here for our staycation. I was going to grab him after our talk," she said.

I smiled. "That's wonderful. Thank you."

"So, tell me what Erin said," she said.

I sat up straighter to give her my good news. "She loved everything. She fell in love with the sanctuary and thinks it's going to help so much. She agreed there are far too many great photos to narrow down. She liked the fishing story and called it quirky." Brynn raised her eyebrow at me, but I waved her off. "Oh, it was exactly what she wanted. More of a personal account of fishing. She did suggest I do a quick article on poaching. In all fairness, she asked me before the poachers showed up and all of this happened." I pointed at my leg.

"Are you writing the entire magazine? She's asking a lot from you."

"I don't mind. *A&A* is short staffed. Besides, this is what I do." I shrugged. "Oh, but the best part?" I paused for dramatic effect.

"Yes?"

"Please don't burn my breakfast." I pointed at the piece of toast that was beginning to smoke in the pan.

"Shit. Okay, that piece is mine. I just got excited. Okay, I promise to pay attention to what I'm doing. Please continue."

I loved the relaxed side of Brynn. The hardness of her eased and made her even more beautiful. I promised that I would do everything I could to keep her happy and not stressed. "So, on top of all of this, she wants me to write a book."

"No way."

I nodded. "She wants me to write a book about how a city girl survived Alaska. After reading my journal and all of my mishaps, she thought it was funny and thinks it would make for a good read."

Brynn abandoned her post and came over to me. She dropped to her knees and kissed me soundly. "That's fantastic, babe. Congratulations." She kissed me again, but this time it was with passion. We were both breathless when we pulled apart. "I don't want to eat two burnt pieces of French toast. I'll be right back." She carried two plates over to the table and I hobbled over to take a seat.

We talked about all of my bad luck until yesterday. I needed to share my experience with her. She was going to have a hard time hearing it, but it needed to be said. When she sat, I started the story.

"After I found out about the book, I wanted to do something special for you. I can't cook for shit, but I can bake a cake. My German chocolate cake is to die for. You're okay with coconut, right?" I asked. She nodded. "So I sent you a text and ran to the store. Oh, I invited Mandy and Lisa over for cake. I guess they know what happened, right?"

"Mandy called me last night after she couldn't reach you. We were already at the hospital so I gave her the scoop."

"Okay. I barely checked my rearview mirror the entire ride back to the cabin. One of the guys must have seen me at the grocery store or talking to Mandy and followed me here. I'm sorry I wasn't more careful."

She brushed it off with a wave of her hand. "Don't even worry about it. I would've done the same."

"He must have called everybody while I was at the store. Ten minutes after I got home, the cabin was surrounded. Lara said she would have officers there in ten minutes. I just needed to hide for that long." Brynn's fingers tightened around her silverware while she listened. "I'm happy you told me about the crawl space. That saved me."

"They still put their hands on you and hurt you," she said.

"Yeah, but I didn't leave with them." I didn't tell her how they dragged me out and slapped me around. I wanted her to think my injuries were crawl space related. She didn't need to know the truth. "Here's an interesting question. Do you know who actually shot me?"

"Lara said it was one of the hunters. You turned and ran away from them, and he took a shot at you. One of the officers shot him. He'll live. The bullet went clean through his right shoulder." She took my plate after I stopped myself from asking for another round even though I was still hungry.

"Do you want more?" she asked. I shook my head. I still needed to watch my caloric intake. "Okay, let me clean up. Do you feel like going with me to collect Wally, or would you rather stay here?"

"I definitely want to go. Let me just throw on a sweatshirt and my boots."

"No rush."

"I miss him. I'm so glad he wasn't here yesterday."

"He's fine. I'm sure he misses you, too. Let's go get him."

CHAPTER THIRTY

Wally was beyond excited to see us. He stood and splayed his paws high while making the strangest noises. "That's the sound he makes when he's happy," Brynn said. That made me tear up. Wally shuffled over to me. I picked him up and tossed him on his back to rub his belly. He grabbed my hands and he wouldn't let go. "Let's get out of here before more people stop us and want to know everything you just went through."

We'd already had a brief conversation with Tina. Since Wally stayed with her last night, I felt the need to inform her. After she heard about my ordeal, she hugged me and was very sweet. I wanted to tell her about the article, but we had time for that later.

"Do we need any medicine or anything while we're out? Because once we get home, I don't want to leave for days. Selfish? Hell yes." Brynn always knew how to make me smile.

"I'm good. Let's go," I said. Wally assumed his position on my lap and looked out the windshield. It was so peaceful in Brynn's truck. Music was playing softly in the background, the sun was shining, and I was sitting next to the woman who changed me. Transformed me for the better. I was happy. The scenery outside was beautiful. Spring was in full force and fishing started next week. I felt like I had been in Alaska for longer than three weeks. Brynn pulled up to the cabin and parked.

"You probably are going to write, aren't you?"

I nodded. "I've been here for a long time and Erin has been accommodating. I want to get this done so you get my undivided attention. If you want to work today, I understand."

"No way. There are things I can do around the cabin. I just want to be around you." Brynn gripped my hand and kissed my fingers. She grabbed Wally from my lap and put him on the ground. They both waited for me to slip out of the truck.

"I will camp out on the couch if that's okay. Do you have a printer I can use?" I couldn't remember seeing a computer anywhere during the tour.

"Yes. Wi-Fi. It's in the back room. Help yourself to whatever you need." She disappeared for a few minutes and came back in sweats and a T-shirt.

We looked like a couple spending the weekend relaxing at home. She sat on the other end of the couch with a book. I printed off Erin's notes and got started. I dismissed lunch with a wave of my hand, missed an early afternoon walk with both of them, and by the time dinner rolled around, Brynn stood directly in front of me and interrupted my flow.

"This is ridiculous. You need to eat something and stretch your legs. We need to dress your wound, and I need you to talk to me for like five minutes."

I'd spent the last five hours writing. Erin asked if she could have the article in three days if I was feeling up to it, but I wanted to get it done tonight. I wanted at least two free days and nights with Brynn. I took my glasses off and tossed them on the coffee table.

"You're right. I need a break. And maybe a massage." I smiled.

"Are you always so focused at deadline time?" she asked.

"Always. But then I get a few days off and it's worth it. I think I'll be done with this sooner than later." Even though I had a lot of information recorded, I needed to verify the laws and run a few things by Lara. We'd been texting the last hour.

"I ordered a pizza. It's going to take a half an hour so I'd like to look at your leg and just talk until it gets here."

I immediately felt guilty. "Yes. Where's Wally?" I didn't remember seeing him this afternoon.

"He's sleeping. Once the pizza gets here, he'll wake up." She sat next to me with her first aid kit and patted her thighs. I lay on my side and put the injured calf on her lap. "Let me know if I'm hurting you." She was so gentle unwrapping it.

"How does it look?" It had been gently throbbing for the last few hours, but I'd been able to distract myself with work.

"Angry," she said.

"Three or four stitches?" I couldn't remember.

"Three." She applied the medication and wrapped it again with fresh gauze and a different wrap. "This will help the bandage stay in place. How are you feeling? Do you want anything stronger than ibuprofen?"

I shook my head. "I really am fine. Tell me about your rescue yesterday. I told you about mine." She smiled and told me about the caribou stuck to a log in the river. It took three rangers to free him. Brody got kicked in the shoulder. He was bruised, but nothing was broken. The buck took off, but Brynn didn't think he was injured.

The delivery boy showed up with dinner and everything was forgotten except eating. Wally even got a few pieces of crust. When I jumped back into the article, Brynn got up, started a fire for us, and sat back down with a different book. It was sweet that she wanted to be near me.

"I'm going to go to bed. You good with Wally out here, or should I take him back with me?" It was ten o'clock and I was almost done.

"He can stay here. He's no bother at all."

"Do you need anything before I go? Medicine? Snacks? A kiss?"

"Yes, no, no, and yes. Definitely yes."

She smiled sadly at me. I sucked for not giving her attention, but I also knew she didn't know what getting this done meant for us. If I finished the article quickly, we would have more time together without the deadline hanging over my head. Also, if I wrote the article well, more people would understand the need for poaching regulations. Hunting laws changed with every presidency, and more and more animals were injured due to lifted restrictions and hunters being careless. This plus the sanctuary article would generate interest and money to help the animals. I was excited to be a part of it.

She kissed me softly. "Don't stay up too late."

I nodded even though we both knew I would. "Good night, Brynn."

It was just past midnight when I sent my article to Erin. There were mistakes, but I had editors to catch the bad stuff. I gave her everything she wanted. My body was sore from the position I was in all day so I stretched for five minutes and drank an entire bottle of water. I was exhausted but I wasn't done. I had one more thing to do before falling asleep.

I crawled into bed behind Brynn. She was on her stomach and even though she looked peaceful, I wanted her awake. I kissed her neck. "I love you," I said against her skin. She stirred. I moved up to her ear and nibbled on her lobe. "I love you," I whispered. "Wake up, love." She muttered something incoherent. I kissed the side of her mouth. "I love you." Her eyelids fluttered open. She blinked awake.

"What?" She closed her eyes again. I wasn't loud enough.

"I love you."

Her eyes stayed open this time. She turned to face me and rubbed her eyes. "What wrong? Are you okay? Did something happen?"

"I said I love you." She stared at me. I said it again and again and sprinkled tiny kisses all over her face. She pulled me in her arms.

"Say it again. I'm not sure I heard you right," she said.

"I told you yesterday, even though I was heavily medicated. I love you, Brynn Coleman. I love how perfect you are in this world and how perfect you are for me. And not just because you were always there for me. You have the purest heart out of anyone I've ever known. I love how much you've changed me. I've found peace with you."

"Oh, Kennedy. I love you, too. So much. And I know I shouldn't because you're leaving any day and I shouldn't open myself to you, but I can't help it. You make my heart beat so fast just with a look or when I hear your sweet laugh. You are a complete mess here in Alaska, but you have made it so much fun to rescue a damsel in distress that I couldn't help but fall for your charm." She pushed me down on the bed and kissed me passionately, deeply, completely. She pushed off my clothes and I did the same with hers. We both moaned when our naked bodies touched.

"You fit me so well. So tall, strong, and beautiful." I ran my hands up and down her body. I would never get enough of her.

She settled between my legs and pushed into me. I was so tired, but a surge of love and passion raced through me and I wanted to show Brynn how much she meant to me. We found our rhythm, but before I could come, she stopped and placed kisses all the way down my body until she reached my core. She moaned at how wet I was for her. I was swollen with need. I only lasted a few minutes with her mouth on me. I was ready to be hers. I cried out as she devoured me. She crawled back up to kiss my mouth and hold me while I rode out each wave of my orgasm. I held nothing back.

"I love you," she said against my mouth.

I kissed her hard and she matched my passion easily. I slid two fingers inside her and moaned with her. She was so tight that I could feel her heartbeat against my fingers. She was mine. We both knew it. I slid in and out slowly, but she begged me to go faster. Still above me, I watched her face as I pumped in and out of her. She leaned down and bit my shoulder. She was keeping herself in check, but I wanted her to let go.

"Come for me." I pressed a kiss into her hair.

She bit harder and pushed back into my hand. I massaged her clit with my thumb. After thirty seconds of build up, she yelled while her body tightened and released her beautiful energy. She lay beside me and put her hand on my chest.

"I really do love you. It's going to be so hard to let you leave in two days," she said. The smile slid off of her face.

I smiled at her. Not just a sweet, normal smile, but the cat-that-ate-the-canary kind of smile.

"You don't have to be so happy about it."

"Hey, you worry too much." I leaned over to kiss her cheek.

"When does Erin want you back?"

I shrugged. "It doesn't matter."

"Kennedy, please tell me when you have to be home. Don't leave me hanging, love." She sounded sad. All I could do was smile at her and touch her.

"Brynn, that's what I've been trying to tell you. I'm already home."

❖

Eight months later

I busted into the cabin, the swirling snow and cold air pushed me through the door faster than I would've liked. "Why am I here?"

"Because you live here, love," Brynn said. She greeted me with a warm kiss, took the groceries from my arms, and kicked the door shut.

"This is brutal. A couple of inches of snow? Like ten inches fell in the twenty minutes I was at the grocery store. How am I going to survive winters here?" Brynn pulled me into her embrace.

"You can hibernate here like a bear. I'll wake you only to feed you and make love to you. I'll do all the shopping and shoveling from now on. Deal?" She kissed me. It was the kind of kiss that reminded me of why I was sharing my life with her. I melted into her.

"Deal. Because it's going to take me a long time before I'm ready to tackle the roads around here by myself." I'd begged Brynn to let me drive to the store that morning. They forecasted only a few inches. It was probably only three inches, but I loved to exaggerate for the attention. Brynn never failed at giving it to me. "I have a surprise for you." She twirled me in her arms so my back was against her chest. She walked me over to a box. "They're here."

I squealed with delight. "They're here." I turned around and kissed her. "They're here," I repeated. She handed me her pocketknife, blade unfolded. I carefully cut the tape along the edges. I opened the flaps and we both stared.

"Beautiful. And brilliant." She was just as excited as I was.

"I wonder if Mandy got her box, too?" I asked. I picked up a copy of my first book, *Does Prada Make Hiking Boots?* The title was over the top, but Erin assured me it was a smash. The pre-order sales were already through the roof.

I had written about everything that happened to me and already had a few stories to put into the sequel I had a contract on. I thought nobody would want to read about my hardships, but I was dead wrong. People liked to read about failures, especially humorous ones, and they loved stories where the protagonist wins. I was a winner all around. I got the girl, a multi-book contract, an Ellie award finalist nod for the sanctuary article, and a pet raccoon named Wally. I had settled into the perfect life for me.

"I love you, Brynn." I kissed her softly and held her close. I loved feeling her heartbeat against my skin.

"I love you more." A laugh rumbled in her chest.

"Impossible." I kissed her again. "I moved thousands of miles to be with you and Wally. You gave me a dresser." I smiled. We both knew I had an entire room that Brynn had converted into a closet for me.

"I gave you a few drawers and my heart."

"I think I deserve more." I kissed her and she smiled.

"Then marry me."

About the Author

Kris Bryant grew up a military brat living in several different countries before her family settled down in the Midwest when she was twelve. Books were her only form of entertainment overseas, and she read anything and everything within her reach. Reading eventually turned into writing when she decided she didn't like the way some of the novels ended and wanted to give the characters she fell in love with the ending she thought they so deserved.

Earning a B.A. in English from the University of Missouri, Kris focused more on poetry, and after some encouragement from her girlfriend, decided to tackle her own book.

Kris can be contacted at krisbryantbooks@gmail.com
Website: http://www.krisbryant.net

Books Available from Bold Strokes Books

Breakthrough by Kris Bryant. Falling for a sexy ranger is one thing, but is the possibility of love worth giving up the career Kennedy Wells has always dreamed of? (978-1-63555-179-2)

Certain Requirements by Elinor Zimmerman. Phoenix has always kept her love of kinky submission strictly behind the bedroom door and inside the bounds of romantic relationships, until she meets Kris Andersen. (978-1-63555-195-2)

Dark Euphoria by Ronica Black. When a high-profile case drops in Detective Maria Diaz's lap, she forges ahead only to discover this case, and her main suspect,aren't like any other. (978-1-63555-141-9)

Fore Play by Julie Cannon. Executive Leigh Marshall falls hard for Peyton Broader, her golf pro…and an ex-con. Will she risk sabotaging her career for love? (978-1-63555-102-0)

Love Came Calling by CA Popovich. Can a romantic looking for a long-term, committed relationship and a jaded cynic too busy for love conquer life's struggles and find their way to what matters most? (978-1-63555-205-8)

Outside the Law by Carsen Taite. Former sweethearts Tanner Cohen and Sydney Braswell must work together on a federal task force to see justice served, but will they choose to embrace their second chance at love? (978-1-63555-039-9)

The Princess Deception by Nell Stark. When journalist Missy Duke realizes Prince Sebastian is really his twin sister Viola in disguise, she plays along, but when sparks flare between them, will the double deception doom their fairy-tale romance? (978-1-62639-979-2)

The Smell of Rain by Cameron MacElvee. Reyha Arslan, a wise and elegant woman with a tragic past, shows Chrys that there's still beauty to embrace and reason to hope despite the world's cruelty. (978-1-63555-166-2)

The Talebearer by Sheri Lewis Wohl. Liz's visions show her the faces of the lost and the killers who took their lives. As one by one, the murdered are found, a stranger works to stop Liz before the serial killer is brought to justice. (978-1-63555-126-6)

White Wings Weeping by Lesley Davis. The world is full of discord and hatred, but how much of it is just human nature when an evil with sinister intent is invading people's hearts? (978-1-63555-191-4)

A Call Away by KC Richardson. Can a businesswoman from a big city find the answers she's looking for, and possibly love, on a small-town farm? (978-1-63555-025-2)

Berlin Hungers by Justine Saracen. Can the love between an RAF woman and the wife of a Luftwaffe pilot, former enemies, survive in besieged Berlin during the aftermath of World War II? (978-1-63555-116-7)

Blend by Georgia Beers. Lindsay and Piper are like night and day. Working together won't be easy, but not falling in love might prove the hardest job of all. (978-1-63555-189-1)

Hunger for You by Jenny Frame. Principe of an ancient vampire clan Byron Debrek must save her one true love from falling into the hands of her enemies and into the middle of a vampire war. (978-1-63555-168-6)

Mercy by Michelle Larkin. FBI Special Agent Mercy Parker and psychic ex-profiler Piper Vasey learn to love again as they race to stop a man with supernatural gifts who's bent on annihilating humankind. (978-1-63555-202-7)

Pride and Porters by Charlotte Greene. Will pride and prejudice prevent these modern-day lovers from living happily ever after? (978-1-63555-158-7)

Rocks and Stars by Sam Ledel. Kyle's struggle to own who she is and what she really wants may end up landing her on the bench and without the woman of her dreams. (978-1-63555-156-3)

The Boss of Her: Office Romance Novellas by Julie Cannon, Aurora Rey, and M. Ullrich. Going to work never felt so good. Three office romance novellas from talented writers Julie Cannon, Aurora Rey, and M. Ullrich. (978-1-63555-145-7)

The Deep End by Ellie Hart. When family ties become entangled in murder and deception, it's time to find a way out... (978-1-63555-288-1)

A Country Girl's Heart by Dena Blake. When Kat Jackson gets a second chance at love, following her heart will prove the hardest decision of all. (978-1-63555-134-1)

Dangerous Waters by Radclyffe. Life, death, and war on the home front. Two women join forces against a powerful opponent, nature itself. (978-1-63555-233-1)

Fury's Death by Brey Willows. When all we hold sacred fails, who will be there to save us? (978-1-63555-063-4)

It's Not a Date by Heather Blackmore. Kade's desire to keep things with Jen on a professional level is in Jen's best interest. Yet what's in Kade's best interest…is Jen. (978-1-63555-149-5)

Killer Winter by Kay Bigelow. Just when she thought things could get no worse, homicide Lieutenant Leah Samuels learns the woman she loves has betrayed her in devastating ways. (978-1-63555-177-8)

Score by MJ Williamz. Will an addiction to pain pills destroy Ronda's chance with the woman she loves or will she come out on top and score a happily ever after? (978-1-62639-807-8)

Spring's Wake by Aurora Rey. When wanderer Willa Lange falls for Provincetown B&B owner Nora Calhoun, will past hurts and a fifteen-year age gap keep them from finding love? (978-1-63555-035-1)

The Northwoods by Jane Hoppen. When Evelyn Bauer, disguised as her dead husband, George, travels to a Northwoods logging camp to work, she and the camp cook Sarah Bell forge a friendship fraught with both tenderness and turmoil. (978-1-63555-143-3)

Truth or Dare by C. Spencer. For a group of six lesbian friends, life changes course after one long snow-filled weekend. (978-1-63555-148-8)

A Heart to Call Home by Jeannie Levig. When Jessie Weldon returns to her hometown after thirty years, can she and her childhood crush Dakota Scott heal the tragic past that links them? (978-1-63555-059-7)

Children of the Healer by Barbara Ann Wright. Life becomes desperate for ex-soldier Cordelia Ross when the indigenous aliens of her planet are drawn into a civil war and old enemies linger in the shadows. Book Three of the Godfall Series. (978-1-63555-031-3)

Hearts Like Hers by Melissa Brayden. Coffee shop owner Autumn Primm is ready to cut loose and live a little, but is the baggage that comes with out-of-towner Kate Carpenter too heavy for anything long term? (978-1-63555-014-6)

Love at Cooper's Creek by Missouri Vaun. Shaw Daily flees corporate life to find solace in the rural Blue Ridge Mountains, but escapism eludes her when her attentions are captured by small town beauty Kate Elkins. (978-1-62639-960-0)

Somewhere Over Lorain Road by Bud Gundy. Over forty years after murder allegations shattered the Esker family, can Don Esker find the true killer and clear his dying father's name? (978-1-63555-124-2)

Twice in a Lifetime by PJ Trebelhorn. Detective Callie Burke can't deny the growing attraction to her late friend's widow, Taylor Fletcher, who also happens to own the bar where Callie's sister works. (978-1-63555-033-7)

Undiscovered Affinity by Jane Hardee. Will a no strings attached affair be enough to break Olivia's control and convince Cardie that love does exist? (978-1-63555-061-0)

Between Sand and Stardust by Tina Michele. Are the lifelong bonds of love strong enough to conquer time, distance, and heartache when Haven Thorne and Willa Bennette are given another chance at forever? (978-1-62639-940-2)

Charming the Vicar by Jenny Frame. When magician and atheist Finn Kane seeks refuge in an English village after a spiritual crisis, can local vicar Bridget Claremont restore her faith in life and love? (978-1-63555-029-0)

Data Capture by Jesse J. Thoma. Lola Walker is undercover on the hunt for cybercriminals while trying not to notice the woman who might be perfectly wrong for her for all the right reasons. (978-1-62639-985-3)

Epicurean Delights by Renee Roman. Ariana Marks had no idea a leisure swim would lead to being rescued, in more ways than one, by the charismatic Hudson Frost. (978-1-63555-100-6)

Heart of the Devil by Ali Vali. We know most of Cain and Emma Casey's story, but *Heart of the Devil* will take you back to where it began one fateful night with a tray loaded with beer. (978-1-63555-045-0)

Known Threat by Kara A. McLeod. When Special Agent Ryan O'Connor reluctantly questions who protects the Secret Service, she learns courage truly is found in unlikely places. Agent O'Connor Series #3. (978-1-63555-132-7)

Seer and the Shield by D. Jackson Leigh. Time is running out for the Dragon Horse Army while two unlikely heroines struggle to put aside their attraction and find a way to stop a deadly cult. Dragon Horse War, Book 3. (978-1-63555-170-9)

Sinister Justice by Steve Pickens. When a vigilante targets citizens of Jake Finnigan's hometown, Jake and his partner Sam fall under suspicion themselves as they investigate the murders. (978-1-63555-094-8)